I0687569

STORIES OF INSPIRATION
Historical Fiction Edition
Volume 1

~

WITH ESSAYS FROM

Frances Brody	Philip Kazan	J.L. Oakley
Elizabeth Brundage	Jennifer Kincheloe	Charles Palliser
Megan Chance	Deryn Lake	Alyssa Palombo
Gary Corby	Deborah Lawrenson	Ann Parker
Glen Craney	Gene Lee	Sue Purkiss
Rosemary Dronchi	Joan Lennon	Celia Rees
Ellen Feldman	Michelle Lovric	Elizabeth Rosner
Suzanne Fox	Sarah McCoy	Steven Saylor
Natalie S. Harnett	James McGee	Sophie Schiller
Bruce Holsinger	Cindy Rinaman Marsch	Cam Terwilliger
Andrew Hughes	Miranda Miller	Janet Todd
J. Sydney Jones	Judith Claire Mitchell	Bob Van Laerhoven
M.R.C. Kasasian	Chris Nickson	Josa Young

AND A PREFACE BY ELIOT PATTISON

UPCOMING FROM STORIES OF YOU BOOKS

Stories of Inspiration:
Mystery Fiction Edition

The Mentor that Matters:
Stories of Transformational Teachers, Role Models and Heroes

The Message that Matters:
Wisdom for the Future from Lessons of the Past

Love, Loss, Legacy, and Life:
Stories from America's Extraordinary Hospices

Heart, Hope, and Healing:
Stories from America's Extraordinary Hospitals

www.storiesofyou.org

STORIES OF INSPIRATION
Historical Fiction Edition
Volume 1

PREFACE BY ELIOT PATTISON

EDITED AND WITH AN INTRODUCTION
BY SUZANNE FOX

STORIES OF YOU BOOKS

STORIES OF YOU BOOKS
Post Office Box 691175
Vero Beach, FL 32969-1175
772.539.2904
www.storiesofyou.org
support@storiesofyou.org

Stories of Inspiration: Historical Fiction Edition, Volume 1

Stories of You Books supports the value of copyright and its role in enabling artists, including writers, to produce creative works that enrich our community and culture and to sustain creative careers. We appreciate your support of authors' rights.

The scanning, uploading, reproduction, and/or electronic or other sharing of any part of this book without permission of the author constitutes unlawful piracy and theft of the author's intellectual property. Other than brief quotations for review purposes, no part of this book may be used without prior written permission of the author of the essay involved. For permissions, please contact the author directly or email Stories of You Books at support@storiesofyou.org.

Book design by cj Madigan

Corridors of Time cover art © RedRemy used under a Creative Commons license

"On the Power of the Historical Novel" © Eliot Pattison 2016

"Forward into History" © Suzanne Fox 2015

All essays in this volume are the copyright of their respective creators and are reproduced here with permission. Page 224, "Copyright and Prior Publication," constitutes an extension of this copyright page.

For information on bulk sales and other special programs, contact Stories of You Books at support@storiesofyou.org.

Dedicated to
readers, writers, and history lovers everywhere

and with heartfelt appreciation for both
our contributing authors and their loyal fans

If history were taught as stories it would never be forgotten.

—Rudyard Kipling

The true alchemists do not change lead into gold. They change the world into words.

—William H. Gass, *A Temple of Texts*

The destiny of the world is determined less by the battles that are won and lost than by the stories it loves and believes in.

—Harold C. Goddard, *The Meaning of Shakespeare*

CONTENTS

ELIOT PATTISON

~

PREFACE

On the Power of the Historical Novel

We have misplaced our history. Studying our past has been dropped from many required curricula in our schools, and our students score lower in history than any other subject—which should come as no surprise to anyone who has turned the sterile pages of modern texts. Those pages squeeze the life out of history, rendering it an arid dump of dates and statistics, as if the story of mankind were just a scientific experiment of interest only to technicians. But we are not composed of dates and data, we are not constructed of factoids to be reduced to graphs and charts. The DNA that makes us possible was bestowed on us by people who lived incredible lives, who endured unspeakable adversities, engaged in staggering adventures, suffered abject tragedies and celebrated boundless joys. We all swim with them in the same great ocean of humankind, separated not so much by beliefs, appetites, and interests as by technology and time.

Stories of our forebears and tales of the struggle to be human have been a vital part of every culture. They are part of our spiritual

DNA, and our institutions have failed us by ignoring them. We are diminished by losing that connection with our ancestors. Our cultural gurus preach self-awareness but how can we be self-aware if we don't even understand the legs we stand on? If you don't know history, novelist Michael Crichton once observed, "you're just a leaf that doesn't know it is part of a tree." We have historical novels because our history books and our history classrooms are just not good enough.

I write and I read historical novels to embrace the richness of the human story. I don't want to simply be told that Marco Polo visited Asia in the 13th century, I want to hear the braying of his camels along the ancient Silk Road and feel his awe as he enters the Chinese capital. Years ago I read a history of early America whose only treatment of the amazing Iroquois Confederation was a timeline that noted its collapse in the mid-18th century. That dismissive note regarding one of the most remarkable cultures of North America lit a slow burning anger that became one reason I began writing novels set in that period. I don't want a vital people reduced to a date; I want to see the tears of Iroquois widows and hear the slow, melancholy beat of their tribal drums. Don't just tell me that Leif Ericsson came to America in 1001, make my eyes sting from the salt spray off the bow of his Viking ship. These people were as alive as you and I. These people became us. Their lives are pages in the human story, the genes that make up that spiritual DNA that survives in all of us. History books are unable to convey that essence, but thankfully, as Emerson reminded us, "Fiction reveals truth that reality obscures." This is the glory, and the duty, of the historical novelist.

Those of us who anchor our work in distant times can sense that glory as we peel away the layers that obscure the past—but we must also feel the responsibilities that come with exploring that truth. That duty isn't simply about being factually accurate. Accuracy and honesty in conveying our settings and characters are vital—without them we not only lose our readers, we damage the genre. But authenticity is about more than just fact checking. Any writer can make a character walk and talk, but only when we know the character's motives, mannerisms, dress, affections, and affectations does he or she come to life. Constructing these elements in a distant day and place is a formidable challenge. It means laborious immersions in the sea of time, but when the author emerges, dripping with insight, the successful translation of setting and character across centuries can be a *tour de force*.

Ultimately, it is such translation that is the real power of historical novels. Without that translation the ancient Japanese tea ceremony becomes just another way to imbibe caffeine. With it, an act of grace and beauty performed hundreds of years ago can still resonate within us. The best historical novels let us swim in the vast human sea, unrestrained by time.

ELIOT PATTISON is the author of eight Inspector Shan mysteries, most lately *Soul of the Fire*. *The Skull Mantra*, which debuted the series, won the Edgar Award and was a finalist for the Gold Dagger. He is also the author of the Bone Rattler mystery series, set in the mid-18th century, and the post-apocalyptic mystery novel *Ashes of the Earth*. An international lawyer by training, Pattison is a world traveler who has spoken and written extensively on international issues. Pattison resides in rural Pennsylvania with his wife, three children, two horses, and two dogs on a colonial-era farm. For more information on the author and books, visit www.eliotpattison.com.

SUZANNE FOX

~

INTRODUCTION

Forward into History

"Write what you know," a familiar guideline for writers advises. It's a rare writer who hasn't heard that maxim a hundred times, but authors of historical fiction ignore it anyway. They don't actually know what it is like to live in Biblical Jerusalem, feudal Japan, Belle Époque Paris, war-torn Dresden, or "Beat" Greenwich Village—much less, say, the Ice Age, the focus of Jean Auel's iconic *The Clan of the Cave Bear*. They are not, and (short of some odd twist of reincarnation) never have been, Tutankhamen, Sappho, Attila the Hun, Empress Wu, Shaka Zulu, "Typhoid" Mary Mallon, or Oskar Schindler, all famous figures who among many others have been the basis for highly regarded historical novels. When an author decides to set a novel in history, she is boldly deciding to write what she doesn't, and by definition can't, fully comprehend.

Therein lie the opportunities, the choices, the challenges, and the fun.

The opportunities, of course, are legion. The past is a treasure trove of moments and personalities, places and situations, images and themes, impressions and tensions: a virtually endless repository, in fact, of the sources of great fiction. Since modern advancements in both travel and technology make the details of the past more accessible to us than ever before, it's not surprising that there has been a flowering of historical fiction in recent decades, or that individual authors in the genre can find their starting points in an astonishing diversity of places. A briefly-glimpsed photo in a book or magazine…a place that reverberates with earlier lives and times, seen just once but never forgotten…the layer upon layer of history in a beloved hometown…a surprising historical fact half-buried in a website or archive…a family document or letter—the past is everywhere, it seems, practically begging novelists to harvest its bounty.

But as the essays in this collection prove, historical starting points are just that: starting points. Their transformation into compelling fiction faces the historical fiction writer with a bewildering array of choices. Some conscious and others instinctive or even visceral, these decisions can take a single idea in a myriad of directions. Will the novel home in on a single place and time, juxtapose one or more periods, or attempt an epic breadth? How much if at all will actual historical events and figures play into the fictional story? Will the voice of the novel adopt or ignore the linguistic conventions of the era? Will the mood be comic or somber, the style literal or impressionistic, the narration trustworthy or tricky? The voice first, third, or even second person? The genre romance, mystery, adventure, fantasy, or some genre-defying combination? Some of these choices are made right at the start; others can only be made, or remade, later on, when the shape of a story has begun to reveal itself.

Even as those decisions are made, the historical novelist faces the challenge of mastering two kinds of historical realities. The first, and by far the easier, has to do with getting the facts right. The precise kind of candles or lamps that lit the homes of Roman, medieval, Tudor, Regency, or late Victorian Britain. The exact weapons that the soldiers of Genghis Kahn, Alexander, Napoleon, Stalin, or the IRA deployed. The proper folds, patterns, and symbolism of an 18th-century geisha's kimono. The specific knowledge a Gold Rush prospector might have about what was happening in his nation's capital, and when and how he received it. I've said that this is the more manageable of the challenges, but that's not to say it's simple. A good historical novel depends on hundreds if not thousands of such details, and it's all too easy to get an awful lot wrong.

Even more difficult are the subtler aspects of the past that a historical novelist needs to evoke: not the facts, but the *feelings* of a past time and place. To make a story real for us, a historical novelist must go far beyond the encyclopedia's charts and chronologies. The lives of fictional characters are no more driven by facts or generalities than the lives of living humans; for every one moment that our lives are shaped by what will become recorded history, there are a hundred moments defined by subtle textures, sensations, impressions, emotions, and assumptions.

And while some of those are timeless, others are not. The chiton worn by the ancient Greeks, for example, would have had its own specific feeling, its own impact on the way the wearer stood and moved and perceived him- or herself, and all of these would be different from the ways we move and feel and understand ourselves in today's blue jeans or business suits. Knowledge about such things is typically found, if at all, in diaries and letters, documents and photographs, rather than history books. Even then, some realities can only be guessed at rather than known: reached by bold and imaginative leaps of faith, rather than dogged reliance on comfortably verifiable sources.

From the musings just offered, you might feel that writing historical fiction is a form of voluntary torture, practiced only by the self-punishing or even the overtly deranged. As a writer myself, far be it from me to claim too much sanity for my peers, much less myself. But as both writer and editor, I can say this: For all its tests and disappointments, for all our writerly griping and complaint, the process of creating historical fiction is fun.

First and foremost, of course, there's the fun of history itself, its dramas and puzzles and surprises, its moods and sights and sounds. Historical novels are time travel, for the writer as well as the reader. Then there's the fun of those starting points....the lure of the how-dids, what-ifs, what-happeneds, whys or why-nots. All novels contain questions that compel their creator, and there's a real delight in pursuing those puzzles to their end.

Finally, of course, there's the fun of being a creator itself—a prime mover, if you will. Writing any kind of fiction involves building worlds, and that kind of imaginative scope and control is always a heady pleasure. Even more satisfying, for historical fiction authors at least, is (re)building the world of a past that we can no longer inhabit except in the imagination. Writing historical fiction, we can live imaginatively in a place and time that puzzles, or fascinates, or moves us. We can enmesh our characters—our proxies, alter egos, secret agents—in all that is richest and most transformative there. We can understand our own present moment through that past, and vice versa. And best of all, of course, we can invite readers to share it all with us, creating a dialogue that, though inspired by the past, is shared in our living present.

Stories of Inspiration: Historical Fiction Edition is designed to offer a behind-the-scenes glimpse of the opportunities, choices, challenges, and fun of crafting historical fiction. The essays within come from a diverse group of British, European, and American writers working in a variety of genres and depicting a wide range of places, people, and periods. In their reflections, we glimpse the exhilaration of the moments when the first glimmer of a story idea seizes the imagination...the wonderfully diverse and unexpected sources from which those starting points can come...the painstaking decisions required to narrow endless possibilities into a single distinct fictional form and narrative...and, sometimes, the wrong turns and revisions that must be faced along the path to a compelling finished work.

Similarities link these stories of inspiration and effort, but differences abound as well. In all their contrast and commonality, the essays celebrate the energy of the imagination, the challenges of the writer's craft, the enduring fascination of history, and the transformative power of the written word to connect places, times, and people.

Whether you are a reader or a writer yourself, I hope the collection will enhance your appreciation of writing, reading, the richness of humanity's past, and the unlimited possibilities of our shared creative future.

Just as important, I hope it will inspire you to seek out at least one of the books discussed within, and enjoy it fully for yourself. Whether it transports you to Pompeii, Paris, or Philadelphia, whether it brings you to laughter or tears, I know it will be a rewarding journey.

Suzanne Fox
Vero Beach, Florida
September 2016

Editorial Note

Like other *Stories of You* books, this anthology was conceived to celebrate the diversity of individual voices. While we have made proofreading and copy-editing alterations in preparing this book for print, we have chosen not to override our authors' personal choices on issues of style. We have, however, changed British spelling and usage to American style norms to allow for a reasonably consistent reading experience from one essay to the next. No disrespect whatsoever is intended to our friends across the (proverbial) pond, or to their glorious "English English," in making these changes.

The limitations of time, the vagaries of author availability, and above all the huge size and variety of the historical fiction marketplace mean that this—indeed, perhaps, any—anthology represents only a small sampling of time periods, places, book themes and situations, author demographics, and so on. Fortuity too plays a role—for example, giving us an unexpected richness of essays discussing books about historical Venice. Outreach for Volume 2 of *Stories of Inspiration: Historical Fiction Edition* begins as this book appears, and we look forward to showcasing more of the range of historical fiction as that and later volumes appear.

FRANCES BRODY

~

Sisters on Bread Street

*B*efore "turning to crime" with my Kate Shackleton 1920s mystery series, I wrote three historical sagas. The setting for these stories was my home city of Leeds in the North of England, and their period spans 1918 to the 1930s. *Sisters on Bread Street* was the first of these novels, inspired by stories told to me by my mother, Julia, or, as we call our mothers in this part of the world, "me mam."

Bread Street, long since demolished, was a cobbled street of densely populated back-to-back houses. The rows on either side were Wheat Street and Apple Street. They sound rural and picturesque, but this was a district for working-class families. Not a tree grew. Not a flower bloomed.

That was where my mother lived with her parents and sister until the girls were orphaned when Julia was age 11 and her sister Dolly 13. They were taken to live with their uncle by marriage and cousins, in a public house near the town center. Uncle Tom was landlord. His wife, my grandmother's sister, had also died.

My mother always wanted to be a writer. On leaving school at 13, she asked a journalist who drank in the pub how she should go about achieving her ambition. He told her she would need a typewriter. That would have been an impossible dream for someone like her.

That she could write, I had no doubt. Whenever we were apart, and after I first left home at 16, we corresponded. She was a wonderful letter writer and also kept diaries.

Eventually, I gave my mother a notebook and asked her to write the story of her life. I had no idea what treasures and what painful memories she would offer. I knew that her mother, Ann, was Irish Catholic and her father a German Jew who had Anglicized his name to Joseph Wood. This did not prevent him from experiencing anti-Semitism. He once had his own butcher shop whose windows were broken by louts. My grandmother was a skilled dressmaker, a talent not inherited by her daughter or by me.

In 1918, 10 days after the German fleet bombarded the northeast coast of England, my grandfather lay in the workhouse infirmary with a fractured skull. He never recovered. His wife had died of appendicitis four months earlier, weeks after giving birth to a son who, without his mother's milk, did not survive.

Such were the bones of Julia's story. She filled notebooks. I interviewed her on tape. My sister and I transcribed her words. I had planned to write one of those slim memoirs that one finds in the local history section of the library. I enjoy such books; capturing the rhythm and detail of lives, they provide a social history that would otherwise be lost, proving that there is no such thing as an "ordinary" life.

The attempt to produce a factual account defeated me. The resulting manuscript did not do justice to my mother's story. "I'm going to write your story as a novel," I told Julia.

"Oh, I thought that's what you were doing," she answered.

The joy of writing fiction is that you can change the story. Tragedy may be held at bay and death postponed. In reality, orphaned Julia and her sister were too young to be actors in their own lives. In fiction, however, I could make them a few years older so that they could become agents of their own destiny. I took the bones of the story—the locations, characters, events and "props" of existence—and performed a conjuring trick.

I was very slow in doing this. By the time I finished the novel, my mother was 99 years old and time was running out. We gave the book its name and chose the cover. I went to a local company, Peepal Tree Press. Peepal generally publishes the work of black and Asian writers. They kindly agreed to print the books for me at a reasonable price and rushed a copy through so that my mother would see it before she died.

She sat in the bay window of her bedroom, book in hand. I expected her to say, "You took your time," or "I thought you'd never do it."

She said, "It reads like a dream." She said, "Will it be a success?" What could I say but "Yes."

Mam and I had our picture in the local paper to mark her hundredth birthday and the completion of the book.

A year to the day after my mother's death, I had a call from my agent, who was at the London Book Fair at the time. She had struck a two-book deal for me. By then, I had expanded *Sisters on Bread Street* to a greater length, exploring the background, developing the girls' stories, and tracing other strands in the tale.

Because *Sisters on Bread Street* had already been published, if only by me, my editor asked me to come up with another title for the commercial publication. I chose *Somewhere Behind the Morning*. The phrase appears in an essay by J.B. Priestley, who wrote, "I have always been delighted at the prospect of a new day, a fresh try, one more start, with perhaps a bit of magic waiting somewhere behind the morning."

With that book and its successor, *Sixpence in her Shoe*, now appearing in new editions, I have reclaimed the title Mam and I chose. Julia once more and forever steps out of the house on Bread Street, delighted at the prospect of a new day.

FRANCES BRODY has written eight mysteries set in the 1920s featuring elegant and intrepid Kate Shackleton, a World War I widow-turned-sleuth. *Murder in the Afternoon* was named a *Library Journal* best book. A 2016 Mary Higgins Clark finalist for *A Woman Unknown*, Frances began her writing career in BBC Radio and Television. She is the author of three sagas. The first saga, *Sisters on Bread Street*, based on her mother's stories, won the HarperCollins Elizabeth Elgin Award. Frances lives in Yorkshire, England, the setting for her novels. Find out more about Frances at www.frances-brody.com.

ELIZABETH BRUNDAGE

~

All Things Cease to Appear

his book started with a house. It was the late '90s and my husband had just joined a medical practice in Troy, New York. For Mother's Day the year before, he took me to a beautiful inn in Columbia County—the Old Chatham Sheepherding Company—and over the course of that weekend I decided that Old Chatham, New York, was one of the most beautiful places on earth and I wanted to live there. We decided to rent a house in nearby Malden Bridge, a historic hamlet that had been settled in the late 18th century. One afternoon, with my girls in the car (our son was just a twinkle in my eye back then) we drove past this old house with a For Rent sign hanging from a tree. It was a lovely white clapboard Cape with a small front porch. I pulled over and we got out. There was nobody around; the place looked empty. We roamed around to the back yard, smelling sage and wild onion, and discovered a Dutch door. On impulse I tried the knob, but of course the door was locked.

And then the strangest thing happened. The bottom half of the door eased open all on its own.

It felt like an invitation. We crawled inside on our hands and knees and the girls, who were three and six at the time, started running wildly through the house as children often do, filling the empty rooms with shrieks and laughter. I was struck by the simple grace of the house, the wide boards, the wavy original glass windows. I couldn't believe the place was empty. We ended up signing a lease and moving in. Shortly thereafter, we discovered that we were not alone. Every morning on the way to school the girls told me stories about the ghosts, three little girls who had died in a fire and whose mother and father were up in heaven. They knew details that seemed beyond their ability to fabricate, including the names of the ghosts, and historic details about an old mill down the road with tainted water. One night, my youngest was literally laughing at something that seemed to be moving around the room. She pointed at it, giggling. I couldn't see it. But I could feel it. I just knew. Months later, when we were moving out, I rushed through the empty house to make sure we hadn't forgotten anything. I opened a cabinet in the built-in corner cupboard of the dining room—for some reason I had never opened it before—and discovered three pairs of children's shoes—little brown leather boots, probably stitched together in the early 1800s, that would perfectly fit those little girl ghosts, matching the ages that my daughters had described. I couldn't help it; I took them with me. It just didn't seem right to leave them there all alone.

We all wonder about death and the mysterious unknown that follows. I knew I wanted to write about the subject and to somehow incorporate a ghost in my story. And then George Clare walked into the cold attic of my brain. He told me he was an art historian with some very deep and troubling secrets. I knew I wanted to set the novel in the Hudson River Valley in the 1970s and I had always loved the painter George Inness, one of the great Hudson River School painters. When I started researching Inness's life, I discovered that he was a devout Swedenborgian. That led me to Emanuel Swedenborg, an 18th-century Swedish philosopher and mystic who believed in the existence of heaven and hell and that, after death, we experience a rich and complex afterlife. This information provided a fascinating subtext and opened up the larger world of the novel, allowing me to pull together the disparate strands of ideas in my head—a horrible, unsolved murder, the ghost of an unresolved woman, three brothers who grow up without her, and a once thriving agricultural community in the throes of urban gentrification.

Building a book is something like building a house. You begin with the land, the type of soil and its history, the landscape. You pour your foundation and construct the frame that will support the floors overhead. In this novel, the foundation is made of the bones of a dead woman, a woman I had read about in a newspaper once, whose murder has never been solved. That dark history cannot be contained in the muddy cellar. It rises up through the old wood boards, seeping out through the cracks, filling the empty rooms. It shouts its terrible story in the faintest whisper.

Dear writer, it says, I beg you: Listen carefully. I have a story to tell.

ELIZABETH BRUNDAGE graduated from Hampshire College, attended NYU film school, was a screenwriting fellow at the American Film Institute in Los Angeles, and received an M.F.A. as well as a James Michener Award from the University of Iowa Writers' Workshop. She has taught at a variety of colleges and universities, most recently at Skidmore College, where she was visiting writer-in-residence. *All Things Cease to Appear* is her fourth novel. She lives near Albany in upstate New York. Find her at www.elizabethbrundage.com.

MEGAN CHANCE

~

The Fianna Trilogy

*T*he decision to write my first young adult series was a complicated one. I really never had any intention to write young adult fiction, known as "YA"—after all, I had an established career in adult historical fiction. The idea for *The Fianna Trilogy* was actually a couple of years in the making, and composed of many different parts.

First, my daughters reached an age where they had started to read a lot of YA fiction, and I began to read it just to see what they were talking about. I admired how no-holds-barred it was, which I didn't expect. That it could be as dark and gritty as adult fiction—and sometimes even more so—appealed to me, and I discovered that the most interesting ideas I'd seen in fiction in years were being written in YA. When you coupled those ideas with deeply emotional conflicts, it was very satisfying, which was something I hadn't felt about adult fiction for some time. Also, I had always volunteered/taught writing classes in my daughters' school, and as they and their friends grew older, they began to ask when I was going to write a book for them.

I began to consider it. Like all ideas, it's the being *open* that matters. Just saying "maybe" is all the subconscious needs. It was no different here. I hadn't decided to write YA; I wasn't trolling for a story idea, and so, naturally, one came to me. Out of the blue, I thought: *What would happen if the gods came back today?* I don't think this is a terribly original question, but it started me thinking. Because I write historical fiction, I wasn't actually very interested in gods returning to a con-temporary world, where they'd probably be thrown pell-mell into an institution. But when I considered it in a historical context, there seemed to be a lot of different possibilities for what might happen to them.

I was also inspired by some other YA books that merged a para-normal/fantasy element with a historical setting, such as Libba Bray's *Gemma Doyle Chronicles*, and similar adult books I'd read in the past, like Anya Seton's *Green Darkness* and Mary Stewart's Merlin Trilogy. I'd always loved reading fantasy, and one can argue that historical fiction is simply another kind of fantasy world. This idea of playing with two of the things I loved, both of which required distinct kinds of world-building, felt challenging and fascinating. It meant that I had to meld the two elements so completely that one could not exist without the other—the legend/fantasy had to mesh seamlessly into a historical framework.

Greco-Roman gods seemed too obvious for the fantasy element. At the time, I'd been researching Druids for another project, and so I decided to explore Celtic mythology. That was when I ran into the Ossianic Cycle, which is a series of tales about the Fianna, ancient warriors who were the elite bodyguards of the High King in Ireland. They were not gods, but some of them were half-gods, or blessed by gods with special gifts. They were led by Finn MacCumhail, and these tales predate the Arthurian legends—some say the tales of Finn and the Fianna are the inspiration for those of King Arthur and the Knights of the Round Table. Many of the same elements exist in both: The Fianna too became greedy and selfish and hungry for power, which led ultimately to their downfall, and like King Arthur in Avalon, the Fenian legends claim that Finn and his men sleep beneath Dublin, ready to come back to aid Ireland at her time of greatest need. They can be called to rise by blowing three times on Finn's hunting horn, the *dord fiann*.

At the same time, I'd been doing a lot of research on immigrants in New York City for my novel *Prima Donna*, and with the Fianna tales in mind, I began looking into the Irish immigrant experience. From the 1840s onward, the Irish began arriving on American soil in such huge numbers that many people joked that there were no more Irish left in Ireland. They came to escape the tyranny of British rule and famine. Those who remained were fomenting rebellion with the aid of Americans sympathetic to their cause. Several attempts to overthrow the British failed. What they really needed was more men, more warriors....

Well, there it was. The reason to call back the Fianna. But what happens when you call ancient Irish warriors to help Ireland, and most of Ireland is in America, which is undergoing its own growing pains, and determined to keep the Irish firmly under heel?

It was just so perfect, the way it came together, and with every bit of research I did, it melded more tightly. Part of this is serendipity, but most comes from deliberately looking for ways to weave two disparate parts into a whole. Taking the legends and determining what in them could be adapted to the historical conflict as it existed was one of the most challenging and exciting aspects of the project. For example, the legend of Cormac's Cup—a mythical object used by the High King to make judgments—was crucial in laying the framework for the mythology. Finding ways to utilize the various talents of the Fianna warriors added complexity and adventure to the plot. Discovering the groups in New York City who were actively organizing to help the Irish throw off English rule gave the story a real-world heft. It was really about determining how history and fantasy played off of and strengthened each other, and also how each could ground the other in emotional truth.

The story of the Irish finding a future in America, paralleled and intertwined with that of the Irish in Ireland, was already a coming-of-age story, and so combining it with a young adult coming-of-age story was not so hard to do. That so much was at stake for the Irish in both Ireland and America meant that I could really hit the larger than life elements of the story and still, hopefully, give them resonance and meaning for a modern reader. That is really what you hope to do as a historical writer, whether you're writing adult or young adult fiction.

$\sim$

MEGAN CHANCE is the critically acclaimed, award-winning author of several novels. Her books have been chosen for Borders Original Voices, Booksense and Amazon Books of the Month, and translated into several languages. Girlposse.com calls her a "writer of extraordinary talent," and Booklist calls her work "provocative and haunting." A former television news photographer with a B.A. from Western Washington University, Megan lives in the Pacific Northwest with her husband and two daughters. Find her at www.meganchance.com.

GARY CORBY

~

The Athenian Mysteries

One of the anomalies of historical fiction is that settings cluster. The historical mystery genre was practically invented when the medieval monk Brother Cadfael made it to our shelves, ably guided by his chronicler Ellis Peters, who was in turn a nom-de-plume for Edith Pargeter. Cadfael was a huge success.

It wasn't long before a small army of imitators had flooded the market with their own historical mysteries, and every single one of them was set in the same place. To look at the list, you would think that the cathedrals and cloisters of England were the medieval murder capital of Europe.

Over time the genre spilled out to other times and places. But it's interesting to see that the cluster effect never went away. There are a lot of mysteries set in Victorian London. Perhaps that's natural with Sherlock Holmes on the premises. Holmes, incidentally, is not historical mystery. When Conan Doyle wrote them, those books were almost contemporary. Meanwhile, in the ancient world, Rome and Roman Britain was the place to be.

The odds are high that if you're reading a historical mystery it is set in one of those three places: medieval England, Victorian London, or Roman Empire. There is a distinct lack of mysteries set in, say, 7th-century Papua New Guinea.

There are exceptions, of course. There is an excellent series set in medieval China starring Judge Dee, written by Robert van Gulik. It is largely ignored. There are terrific books set in the Aztec period and among the Mongol Hordes. They too have trouble getting attention. There are, however, minor success stories in ancient Egypt and in the Byzantine period.

I have a theory as to why this is.

The times and places that readers relate to are the ones that led to the world we live in. Most historical mystery readers live in what, for want of a better term, I will call the tradition of Western European civilization. Rome and medieval Europe are indisputable ancestors; medieval China less so. This also explains why ancient Egypt does okay. It might not be in a direct line to us, but Egypt has long fascinated. Just walk into the Louvre or the British Museum to see how much Egypt calls to us. The Byzantine period likewise.

If my theory is good, then there are other times and places that should also ring the bell for readers. I thought about this very carefully when I created my own series, and then I wrote the Athenian Mysteries, set in classical Greece.

The Golden Fifty Years of Greece was the birth of Western civilization. It was the birth of democracy, of trial by jury, of science and philosophy and of written history. Herodotus, who wrote the first book of history, is even one of my characters.

When I wrote that first book, I was essentially testing the idea that we like the times and places that created our world. As I write this, the sixth book of the Athenian Mysteries is released, the seventh is written, and I am starting on the eighth. The theory looks good. Either that, or I am very lucky!

Mysteries set in Renaissance Italy should do very well, for exactly the same reason. There are some books set then, but I feel this is a period that hasn't been mined as much as it deserves.

The Napoleonic era should be a natural. It is certainly a natural for war stories. One point though is that murder mysteries flourish more in times of political maneuver, plotting and conspiracy, rather than outright conflict. Despite which, there is a growing field of World War II mysteries. There are plenty of people still with us who lived through that—such as, for example, my own mother—despite which it probably counts for historical mystery. I better not tell my mum.

Even as I wrote this essay, it occurred to me that Charlemagne's empire would be a fun choice for murder and mayhem. Plus you would get to have knights doing knightly deeds. What this amounts to is that the opportunities for historical mystery almost outweigh the number of people writing them, and there are plenty of places to travel to that are largely untapped.

Readers love it when the story includes historical people that they already know. It isn't essential to have such characters, but it helps. My detective hero Nico is the elder brother of an irritating lad named Socrates. Nico works for an up-and-coming young politician by the name of Pericles. You already know about Pericles and Socrates; at the very least you read about them at school. I put flesh and personality on those ancient guys, and give them a chance to breathe, and they repay me by making the story more real.

Let me mention where the information comes from, for any historical mystery, especially finding the details of everyday life. I can only talk about how I myself go about doing book research, but I know many authors who follow the same process that I do.

Original sources are essential! I can't emphasize that enough. For classical Greece a decent knowledge of the histories written by Herodotus and Thucydides is mandatory. They're the Big Two, and as a writer if you don't know them then you are doomed. My copies of their books are within arm's reach, even as I write this, on the shelf above my head. If you're the reader, however, then your obliging author is doing the research for you, and distilling it into a fun story.

I enjoy book research. I enjoy it so much that it's hard to stop. Herodotus is a fine old chatterbox and reads more like a Boys' Own Adventure than the founding document of history and anthropology. Thucydides is full of geopolitics and is better than any modern thriller. Both can be mined mercilessly for material. There's a novel on every page. For example, you may have heard of a movie called *300*. It comes from Herodotus, seriously mangled.

The same logic applies to *every* period. It's so important to read the words of the people who were there.

It's surprising how much information about daily life comes from archaeology and not written history. What if your character is in Athens in 460 B.C. and needs to take out the garbage? People at the time never thought to write down where they dumped their rubbish.

Archaeologists find the middens, so we know most people kept a dump out back. We get house plans, cooking utensils, boat design, weaponry, clothing pins, bronze mirrors, hair combs, assorted pottery, voting tokens, clothing styles, musical instruments, and all sorts of other stuff from archaeology. The Metropolitan Museum, the Louvre, the British Museum and the National Archaeology Museum of Athens are my friends.

These then are the essentials of time and place: periods that are relevant to the lives of readers; times of intrigue; real people of interesting personality; original sources; and archaeology to tell us about them.

When you put them together what you get is fun.

~

GARY CORBY is the author of the long-running Athenian Mystery series, starring Nicolaos, his girlfriend, Diotima, and his irritating 12-year-old brother, Socrates. Gary lives in Sydney, Australia, with his wife, two daughters, two ducks, two budgerigars, and a brush turkey that is almost as irritating as Socrates. He blogs at www.garycorby.com on all things ancient, Athenian, and mysterious.

GLEN CRANEY

The Fire and the Light

*M*any readers are fascinated by how authors find the ideas for their historical novels. When I tell them my characters choose me, they assume I'm speaking metaphorically.

But no, the inspiration for my books often comes in dreams—not the usual mishmash of subconscious dross, but in lucid sleep visions that are vivid, rich in emotional feeling, and studded with symbols, names, and images. The experience is like having one's brain downloaded with a compressed digital file that must be unzipped to decode its message.

The first time this happened, I had an intense dream of a robed woman walking toward me across the ruins of a mountain castle. I heard the word "crusade" chanted while the letters "Mallorca" flashed below this scene. Around the woman's feet sprouted dozens of crosses that shifted between possessing two and three horizontal beams. These crosses seemed to mark the location of forgotten graves. I was struck by their resemblance to the logo used by the American Lung Association in its modern crusade against tuberculosis.

The woman, bathed in a lucent white radiance, beckoned me with outstretched arms and pleaded, "Peace, child, let the Light." Then, I awoke with a start and wrote it all down.

The next morning, I hurried to the library to find out what I could about these strange crosses. The medieval papacy, I discovered, had claimed possession of the triple cross for reasons that remain shrouded in mystery. According to the esoteric classic *Meditations on the Tarot*, one who wields the triple cross is empowered to regulate spiritual respiration between the angelic and earthly realms.

The double cross—also known as the Cross of Lorraine—had been carried by the Knights Templar on their first journey to the Holy Land. Only decades later did those crusading monks replace it with their splayed cross *pattée*. Hermeticists would later adopt the double cross as a symbol to denote their primal law: As above, so below. During World War II, the French Resistance embraced the Cross of Lorraine as a rallying insignia in its struggle against the Nazi occupation. Today, this cross can be seen painted on walls in southwestern France in a call for the return of independence to the region once known as Occitania.

Several weeks into my research, I met the late Dr. Norma Lorre Goodrich, a scholar of myth and ancient religions from Claremont College. In her book *The Holy Grail*, she identified the triple cross as a medieval watermark called the Catharist Cross. Yet that symbol had nothing to do with the crucifixion. Instead, it had been known since ancient times as the "Cross of Light" that depicted the rays of the spiritual sun.

I began to wonder if the Vatican had confiscated this triple cross after exterminating the medieval Cathars, a sect of pacifist healers. The alternating number of traverse beams on the crosses in my dream suggested a connection between these doomed heretics and the recurring struggle for freedom in France. Although raised a Roman Catholic, I had never been told of the Albigensian Crusade, the 13th-century war of extermination sanctioned by the Church. Yet as my investigation into these pacifist Christians deepened, I couldn't shake the feeling that my mysterious muse had brought a warning for our own time, plagued as it is by religious intolerance and terror.

Months later, I was climbing the heights of Montsegur in the Ariege region of France. That desolate mount and its haunting castle ruins looked strikingly similar to the landscape in my dream. And that encounter would prove to be only the first of many *déjà vu* experiences I would have in Cathar country.

A noblewoman named Esclarmonde de Foix once owned Montsegur. She was the sister of the Count of Foix, an enemy of the Church's crusade commander Simon de Montfort. The Viscountess Esclarmonde became a revered Cathar leader and participated in public disputations against the papal legates, including the future St. Dominic. Her influence grew so dangerous that Pope Innocent III publicly condemned her in Rome.

And I found this: The name Esclarmonde means "Light of the World."

But what about the word "Mallorca" that appeared in my dream? While in France, I learned that the House of Aragon held land in the region of old Occitania known as the Kingdom of Mallorca. The old Mallorcan fortress still stands in Perpignan. And the Balearic island of Mallorca, now part of Spain, was a haven for Cathar refugees. A few decades after the capitulation of Montsegur, a female descendant of the extended Perella family from Foix married James, the King of Aragon and Mallorca. After the Church's crusaders killed his father, the Knights Templar raised young James in Aragon. His new queen came from Foix—and her name was also Esclarmonde.

Intrigued by these many references to the Esclarmondes, I consulted Dr. Goodrich's works again. The professor had championed the theory that Viscountess Esclarmonde and her family of Cathar women from Foix were the Grail priestesses sung about secretly by the Occitan troubadours during the 13th century.

The Fire and the Light: A Novel of the Cathars was the result of my quest. Since that first novel, I've had similar initiatory dreams that led to *The Spider and the Stone: A Novel of Scotland's Black Douglas* and *The Virgin of the Wind Rose: A Christopher Columbus Mystery-Thriller*.

Even with such inspiration from the muses, we mortals are ultimately left to the hard work of getting the words down. For me, the key step in the alchemy of historical fiction is the sifting and shaping of the research into a seamless narrative. Having studied Jungian psychology, I search for the path of the hero's journey and the classic archetypes. Having worked in the film business, I've written several of my novels first as screenplays, and I tend to see chapters in my novels as movie scenes. Each story has a unique form that demands to emerge. The most effective historical novelists develop the acumen of the sculptor who perceives the statue in the unhewn block.

GLEN CRANEY holds graduate degrees from Indiana University School of Law and Columbia University Graduate School of Journalism. He practiced trial law before joining the Washington, DC, press corps to cover national politics and the Iran-Contra trial for *Congressional Quarterly* magazine. The Academy of Motion Pictures Arts and Sciences awarded him the Nicholl Fellowship prize for best new screenwriting. He is also a two-time indieBRAG Medallion Honoree, a Chaucer Award First-Place Winner for Historical Fiction set during the Middle Ages, and has three times been named a *Foreword Reviews* Book-of-the-Year Award Finalist. His novels have taken readers to the Scotland of Robert Bruce, to Portugal during the Age of Discovery, to the trenches of France during World War I, and to the American Hoovervilles of the Great Depression. He lives in southern California. His website is www.glencraney.com.

ROSEMARY DRONCHI

~

The Rossini Trilogy

ven in high school, I loved to read about Prohibition, the Crash of 1929, and the struggles of the Depression. So the choice of timeframe for my Rossini novels was an easy one. As for the Mafia element of my stories, that came in part from family legend.

I'm an American of Italian heritage—and very proud of that. So let me say that the more corrupt and violent practices in which some of my Italian characters engage are based in historical reality, rather than intended as any reflection on the character of Italians and their country generally!

My grandfather, Agostino Belcastro, lived with us when I was a child. He was a fascinating man who told many stories of life in the Old Country. Years later, I thought of the stories he told, the way he carried himself, the way people admired him and asked him for assistance. He became a great study for a character.

Even now, I can remember him so vividly. My family lived on Madison Avenue in Albany, NY, on the second floor of a three-story house. It was across the street from St. Anthony's Catholic Church, which my family attended. Every morning, my grandfather would dress in a three-piece suit, white shirt and tie, and polished shoes. He wore a fedora, never went out without his gold pocket watch, and carried a cane with a brass handle. He would sit in front of the house while people came to him. They'd kiss his hand and whisper to him; he would nod, and then someone else would come by.

At noon sharp, he always climbed the stairs to our home, removed his jacket, and sat down to lunch. He would take a full hour to enjoy the meal and then have a two-hour nap, after which he would go down to the street again. Most of the time he found people there waiting for him. He had dinner from five to seven and then was downstairs again, speaking with people, until eleven or twelve. Though I didn't understand it at the time, it now seems clear that he approached his dealings with the people that sought him out like a job. I don't know whether he had actual Mafia connections. But there is no doubt that people approached him as one does a person with power, and that some folks walked on the outside of the street to avoid him.

Like my grandfather, my mother had a lot of tales to share. She was the oldest of six, so she saw a lot as a child. As an adult, she owned and cooked for a prominent Italian restaurant. She served politicians, gamblers, and, I have no doubt, members of the Mafia. When something went down, nine times out of ten it had been hatched at her restaurant. She clearly heard things she wasn't meant to hear, but she was naïve enough that I don't think she realized it... or smart enough to forget what she had heard.

The lives of two of my grandfather's sons—my mother's brothers—also influenced the Rossini story. They ran whiskey from Canada, owned a bar called Club Havana, gambled, and did a lot of other things that broke the law. Happily, according to my mother, they never killed anyone!

My novel evolved in ways I never expected. The more I wrote, the more memories of my grandfather's and mother's stories became vivid. I actually began my first book with Agostino at 76 years old, reading journals his mother and father had written. In genre, that original draft was a family saga, based on my grandfather's life and titled *The House of Batista*. When I started taking writing courses, I was told that it had no excitement or story line and that I needed to spruce—and spice!—it up. Then I took a class with thriller writer David Hagberg. With the confidence of a true expert, he said that the best thing would be to abandon the book.

That was a pivotal moment. The thought of 10 years of work and 586 pages down the drain was painful. But if I wanted to work with someone of David's caliber, I had to change. Reading his novels, I knew it was worth it. It was so clear that his writing had a kind of power, emotional force, and suspense that I needed to learn.

Ten years after that turning point, *Blood Feud* became print. My hope is that it and the other books of the Rossini Trilogy keep the heart of the family material I started with but add the excitement and drive of historical suspense fiction.

Much of the research for the series comes from books and the Internet. But I have also traveled to Italy and seen many of the locations adapted for the story. A villa in Positano—words can't describe its beauty—became the Hotel Rossini. And I've had the good fortune to visit the seaside town of Marina de Gioiosa Ionica, where my grandparents lived and my mother was born.

It was an amazing experience to visit this town, particularly with my husband, daughter, and grandchildren beside me. I found the house where my grandmother was born and walked the blocks of connected houses where she must have walked. Twenty or thirty people heard about the American family looking for a grandparent's home and came out of their stone houses to see us. They knew all about my family—the names of my aunts, uncles, and cousins. It was unbelievable. Yet not one of them invited us in or offered refreshment, which is very unlike the usual Italian tradition of hospitality. Later, I learned that they were afraid I had come back to claim property—whether it was the house, money or something else, I don't know. But I'm sure that if I looked into it more deeply, there was something they were hiding.

While I was exploring, I literally bumped into an elderly man who claimed that my grandmother was his mother. If that was true, I told him, then Agostino Belcastro must be his father. With that, he made a nasty jest and turned his back on me. If I'd had any doubts that my grandfather was more than just a proper old gentleman, that would have banished them.

~

ROSEMARY DRONCHI is the author of the Rossini Trilogy novels: *Blood Feud*, which appeared in 2012; *Retribution*, published in summer 2014; and the upcoming *Redemption*. In addition to the Trilogy, her works include a number of short articles, the award-winning short story *Play for Keeps*, and the contemporary novel *Of Body and Soul*, published under the pen name L.J. Valentine. A professional hairstylist for most of her working life, Rosemary used the stories of her Italian family as inspiration for the novels. Though both grew up in Albany, NY, Rosemary now lives with her husband Tony in Vero Beach, FL, where she has recently retired from owning the Park Place Salon & Spa. Find her online at www.rossinitrilogy.com.

ELLEN FELDMAN

Terrible Virtue

ooks are writers' children. Asked which is our favorite, we scrupulously reply, I love them all. Asked which gave us the most difficulty, we say each had its challenges and rewards. But I'm going to break with custom here. Of the several novels I've published, *Terrible Virtue*, based on the life of Margaret Sanger, was the hardest to write. It also had the longest gestation period, ten years from first inspiration and early research to publication.

I gave up in despair and abandoned the book once, twice, a third time. I could not bring Margaret Sanger to life on the page, but Margaret Sanger would not let me go.

The day I tossed it out for the first time, or at least put it in the dormant file, I ran into a friend. When he asked how I was, I confessed that I had just given up on more than two years of work. He was so appalled that he told the story at a dinner party that evening, and for several weeks I got calls and e-mails of condolence. They were kind, but they didn't make me feel any less a failure or a traitor. I was deserting a friend I had lived with, intensely and intimately, for two years. After writing another novel in the interim, I tried again. A year later, I put the novel aside a second time. Would I never learn, I chastised myself, and once again turned my hand to another book. The third time I returned to the idea and again failed, I was furious at myself for throwing good months and years after bad. Why couldn't I relinquish this obsession, which clearly was ill-conceived?

The answer to why I couldn't give up the book is the same as the answer to why I was having so much trouble writing it—Margaret Sanger, her singular genius, her towering achievements, and her maddening contradictions. How do you bring to life a woman who was at once selfish and altruistic; loyal and ruthless; arrogant and insecure; devoted to improving the lot of all women and fiercely competitive with other women; determined to expose society's hypocrisies and a maker of her own myths; a breaker of sexual taboos who somehow managed to maintain a spotless public persona; a woman who married twice, but didn't believe in marriage, and had countless affairs to prove it; a mother who loved her children but was hopeless at caring for them, and endured the worst heartbreak a parent can know?

It would have been demanding enough to capture this charismatic larger-than-life character in a biography; it was daunting to try to penetrate her mind and heart, which any successful novel must do. But the near impossibility of the endeavor is what attracted me in the first place. As a young woman, I had admired Margaret Sanger and her triumphs, but the more I read about her, the more her incongruities confounded me, and the more determined I became to try to figure out what made this towering figure tick. For that only fiction will do. And in fiction, perhaps more than in any other literary form, what we leave out is as important as—perhaps more important than—what we put in.

Therein lay the key to writing Margaret Sanger. I had been ad-hering too closely, not to the facts—I was determined to stick to those, and I have—but to the minutia of Sanger's life. I was sacrificing the essence of the woman to the details of her existence. I was losing the magic of the individual to the particulars of her struggles, strat-egies, marriages, affairs, and encounters with her children. I had become a bore on the subject of Margaret Sanger rather than a novelist bringing to life her indomitable spirit. When I realized that, when I took a step back to see Margaret Sanger whole, she began to come alive in my imagination and on the page.

I have lived with Margaret Sanger for a decade. Even when I was writing about other characters and times and places, she occupied a corner of my mind. I can't say she is always sympathetic, but I can say she is superb company—exhilarating, inspiring, passionate, brilliant, capable of great love and petty hate, canny about her cause but often blind about her personal life, and always deeply human. She is, in the end, the woman who not only wrought a major social revolution but, more than any other single person, fashioned the sexual landscape we inhabit today.

And here's a footnote to the story behind the book. While I was doing the research for *Terrible Virtue*, I had a recurrent surreal sen-sation. The contemporary headlines I was reading with my morning coffee were uncannily similar to those of a century ago that I was unearthing in libraries and archives. The experience made me realize that from her opening of the first, then illegal, birth control clinic in America in 1916 through her founding of Planned Parenthood to her role in helping develop the Pill in the 1960s, Sanger's story is alive with yesterday's struggles and as timely as today's headlines.

ELLEN FELDMAN, a 2009 Guggenheim fellow, is the author of *Terrible Virtue, The Unwitting, Next to Love, Scottsboro* (shortlisted for the Orange Prize), *The Boy Who Loved Anne Frank* (translated into nine languages), and *Lucy.* She writes both fiction and social history, has published numerous book reviews, and has lectured extensively around the country and in Germany and England. Ellen grew up in northern New Jersey and attended Bryn Mawr College, from which she holds a B.A. and an M.A. in modern history. After further graduate studies at Columbia University, she worked for a New York publishing house. Ellen lives in New York City and East Hampton, NY, with her husband and a terrier named Charlie. Find Ellen online at www.ellenfeldman.com.

SUZANNE FOX

~

The Shell House

*I*n the early 2000s I made some of my living as a ghostwriter, a suitably odd term for a really odd job. One of my projects brought me now and again to the upscale summer enclave of New York's Hamptons, where I would stay at the home of a wealthy designer while working on her book. An inveterate traveler with a discerning eye, she had a distinctly "more is more" philosophy; the 20,000-plus square feet of her house and the equally expansive gardens around it were chock-full of extraordinary things. It was a strikingly beautiful place, if also one where it was hard to feel at ease.

One summer evening, my client and her husband hosted a large dinner party. The guests, Manhattan movers and shakers all, were neither uninteresting nor unkind. But the term "ghostwriter" had rarely felt more apt. Even as I chatted and mingled I felt spectral, insubstantial. I was of their world and yet not of their world—not quite visible and, in the metrics that mattered most in those circles, not quite real.

Those of us who turn to books for comfort as children never entirely lose the habit. Feeling the strain of the cocktail hour, I walked with what I hoped passed for nonchalance to an antique desk in front of a wall of bookshelves. On its glossy surface an art book lay open, a magnifying glass weighting its spread pages. The photograph on the open recto page was an oblique view of a small staircase, its wall curved as though it rose in a turret or tower. The fan of steps near the bottom and the oriel window above were unremarkable. But the walls between were lined with seashells, a riot of colors and shapes and patterns. Not a single inch of undecorated surface was visible except on the glass of the window and the treads of the stairs.

In a moment of jolting intensity, a kind of falling in love at first sight, that image seized my imagination. Out of my first impressions I remember only *obsession* and *fairy tale* and *why* and *a shell within a shell*. That last idea expanded to *shells are houses and houses are shells* before a fellow guest came over to talk to me. Five minutes earlier I would have been grateful for the rescue. Now I felt grudging, and wished he would leave me alone with my thoughts.

I knew from that first moment that I would write a novel based on that shell-lined staircase. Back home in Florida I did some Internet searching for it. I found that it was part of a late 18th-century house called A La Ronde, built by two cousins—"spinster cousins," as most accounts put it—in Devon. A sixteen-sided structure now held by Britain's National Trust, A La Ronde was, and is, filled not just with shellwork but also with a trove of the cousins' possessions, each collection and creation quirkier than the next.

The more I read about them the more interesting Jane and Mary Parminter seemed. I wished that a biography or book had been written about them, but I didn't want to write that book or even a fictionalized account of their lives. Instinct told me that my story would be focused not on two women but one—I named her Claire Hetton—and that the action would take place in the 1850s, a period that fascinates me. My novel pays homage to the Parminters only indirectly, in references to "the Misses," the long dead great-aunts who built the house to which Claire moves and whose resourceful spirit is very much present there. But I kept the shellwork, the unusual tower-like house, and its location not far from the coast. Just as importantly—to my own vision of the story, at least—I embraced the themes of female friendship, art-making and collaboration that the cousins' lives and work suggested.

The mosaics of A La Ronde use over 25,000 shells, definitely not a supply collected from casual strolls on the Devon shingle. The logistics of the shellwork brought another milieu into the novel: the commercial and mostly masculine world of the Victorian trade in natural specimens. From it and its center in London the book's second protagonist, Jonah Reed, was born.

At about the time Jonah entered my scenes in progress, most of my forward motion on the book stopped. By the end of the year in which I first glimpsed that photo of A La Ronde, two Category-5 hurricanes had made landfall in my Florida town and two close family members were struggling with cancer. Over the next decade I helped with caregiving in two states, rebuilt the parts of my house that had been destroyed in the storms, dealt with both of my parents' deaths within the space of twelve months, emptied out their longtime home, and tried to maintain some semblance of a career. Even mustering the energy to earn a living was difficult. Sustained, productive work on a complex novel felt impossible. I worked on the book I was calling *The Shell House* when I could and tried not to blame myself too fiercely when I couldn't.

I might not have been working on the novel, but it was still working on me. When all hell broke loose in 2004, I had a situation and some imagery but not a story. *A young woman moves to a strange round house and makes shell mosaics.* Then what? So what? The answers, it turned out, were not at A La Ronde. They were in my own life and, even more powerfully, in my own losses.

How do we make peace with death and its legacies, from deep longing to a sense of things unsaid or unresolved? Where is the balance best struck between what we owe our families and what we owe ourselves? When do our defenses against pain or loss become so well-crafted—so beautiful, even—that they harden into a shell that confines as much as it protects? The converging stories of Claire Hetton and Jonah Reed could not be more different from my own, but all three trajectories are shaped by similar questions.

I joke that this novel has taken me a reasonable four years to write; it just happens to be four years spread out over fourteen. In the moments my progress on it seems humiliatingly slow, I sometimes remember the image that started me on this work, that photo of the steps at A La Ronde. Choosing the shells, devising the patterns, and getting the mosaic on those curving walls wasn't quick work, even before impediments like corsets are factored into the process. And how right it seems that the staircase was designed not as a straight line but as a spiral like a nautilus shell's, an organic and patient arc.

Author, book consultant and publisher SUZANNE FOX is the creative director of Stories of You Books and the founder/editor of the online journal *Society Nineteen*, which interviews contemporary authors writing about 19th-century experience. Her books include the memoir *Home Life: A Journey of Rooms and Recollections*, which was published by Simon and Schuster and selected as an Editor's Choice by the *Chicago Tribune*, and women's fiction that has been published under two different pseudonyms and translated into seven languages. A frequent teacher and speaker on writing, stories and creativity, Suzanne earned her M.F.A. from Columbia University and is currently working on a novel set in 19th-century Britain. Find out more at www.storiesofyou.org and www.bookstrategy.com.

NATALIE S. HARNETT

~

The Hollow Ground

hile I was a young child my grandfather lived in the Poconos region of Pennsylvania. I grew up in Queens, New York, but I went to northeastern Pennsylvania a lot and I really consider it a second home. Through my grandfather, I got to know the city of Carbondale. We've all seen towns like it— towns that were booming, thriving places before the industries that supported them shut down. You can feel the loss and the depression in things like the abandoned stores with the names still visible above them. There was something about Carbondale's steep, narrow streets and beautiful, large and often dilapidated homes that always called to me. I remember seeing one that had an air conditioner stuck into this gorgeous stained glass window. So it was all the way back in my childhood years that my desire to write about Carbondale formed, but it wasn't until years later that I had the inspiration for the story I would set there—or, actually, in Barrendale, as I called it in *The Hollow Ground*.

At heart, *The Hollow Ground* is about family—that's what I always write about. Brigid, the narrator of the novel, came from several different starting points. My previous novel had been written in the third person voice and I knew that I wanted to try a first-person narrative, to do something different than I'd done before. I also wanted to write about a young girl who has some of the memories, and the kind of wisdom, that my mother has. Her memories of childhood are not overtly similar to Brigid's, but they have both overcome difficult childhoods to become loving, forgiving women.

The experiences of two friends who came from broken homes influenced my sense of that story as well. I've often imagined what it would have been like to grow up with neglectful or abusive parents rather than loving ones. The journey Brigid undergoes with her parents, with her "Ma" especially, is inspired by the process my friends underwent as they moved through hurt and anger to forgive their mothers. That was the framework of the novel, what I was trying to do when I started writing the book.

For me, Brigid's mother is the most powerful character in the book. I could probably write several more novels about her. Her story came into focus as I was reading interviews with old Pennsylvania miners. In one of them, a man in his late 80s told the story of how his mother died when he was six. His father quickly remarried, and his stepmother gave his sister away to an orphanage but "kept" him. He never heard from her again. Even at the age of 86 he started to cry as he talked about it. I was stunned by that, by the thought of what happened to that girl and what her life must have been like. I remember that I was in my back yard in the summer, reading through these interviews and struggling to figure Ma out. Suddenly I just knew that there was her backstory.

My great-grandmother had been sent to an orphanage by her father shortly after her mother died, which I think made me especially sensitive to the story of the old miner's sister. Did that young girl know where she was being sent? What was her last moment at home like? Years later, what was she able to remember of her family? Who did she become as an adult?

The final member of the trio of women in the story is Brigid's grandmother. Gram's strength and resourcefulness really came from my own grandmother, but her stories and manner came from one of my grandfather's neighbors in the Poconos. So did the fictional Gram's experience in the underwear mill.

I had almost a full draft when I remembered my grandfather's neighbors telling me about underground coal mine fires in Scranton. The fires sunk the homes, poisoned people, made the floors of the houses too hot to walk on. It struck me then what an incredible image and metaphor that was. I thought, *why don't I have the family in one of those Scranton fire homes as the story opens, then move them to Carbondale?* But as I went to research the Scranton fires I found almost nothing about them. Instead, I kept reading about fires in Centralia. Trying to get the research on the novel done—something that gained even more urgency once I got pregnant—I went to the Carbondale Historical Society. As my mom and I were going through their records, I came across information about an intense coal fire in Carbondale itself. I remember sitting there, looking at that room and the window with the light coming through it, and realizing that I just had to tell that story—and to completely rewrite the novel.

Since the book appeared I've done events in Pennsylvania and New York and beyond. So many of the stories I've heard along the way have been of experiences much worse than what I depicted in the novel. I've felt at times that I wished I could make changes to the book, but I'm not sure it could have sustained the reality of how bad the fires really are.

Personal stories from people who have experienced the fires have a life—a value—of their own. Most people, even those from the Northeast, have never heard of the coal fires. But there are over 50 burning in Pennsylvania alone. Every coalmine state has this issue; every country with coalmines has this issue. The memories people share about it are incredibly moving and worthy of attention—as human stories, and because they shine a powerful light on the environmental and economic disasters we can cause.

NATALIE S. HARNETT has an M.F.A. from Columbia and has been awarded an Edward Albee Fellowship, a Summer Literary Seminars Fellowship, and a Vermont Studio Center Writer's Grant. Her fiction has been a finalist for the Mary McCarthy Prize, the Mid-List Press First Series Award for the Novel, the Glimmer Train's Short Story Award for New Writers, and The Ray Bradbury Short Story Fellowship. Her work has appeared in the *Chicago Quarterly Review*, the *Irish Echo*, the *Madison Review*, *The MacGuffin* and the *New York Times*. Her debut novel, *The Hollow Ground*, won the 2015 John Gardner Fiction Book Award and the 2014 Appalachian Book of the Year Award and was long-listed for the 2016 International Dublin Literary Award. She lives in Long Island and Northeastern PA with her husband and child. Find out more at www.natalieharnett.com.

BRUCE HOLSINGER

The John Gower Novels

ne of the paradoxes of historical fiction is that it must both inhabit and invent its settings. Writers in the genre might perform months of research, pore through a dozen archives, spend weeks walking the back roads and visiting the buildings and streets that once defined their characters' lives. Yet no matter how much research we perform, no matter how often we travel to the cities, towns, and landscapes portrayed in our fiction, we are faced, in the end, with the difficult task of invention—of making all or most of it up. When it comes to place, even the most rigorously researched historical novel demands creative license, as we flesh out in language those intimate details of structure, landscape or room we can never fully recover from the archive.

Every historical place and time, though, comes with its own unique set of challenges, as I've learned in writing novels set in late medieval London, during the reign of Richard II. The post-medieval history of the city proved all but catastrophic for anyone wishing to place a novel in that world. The built environment of medieval London is largely lost to us, victim of the Reformation, the Great Fire of 1666, the Blitz, and the sheer passage of time. The great Roman walls, which once circumscribed the Square Mile and defined the core of pre-modern London, were dismantled centuries ago, and while certain streets retain their medieval names, these byways are deceptive guides indeed to the ambience and sightlines of the 14th-century city.

There are numerous traces of medieval London and its environs if you know where to look for them, though, and one of the great pleasures in researching and writing *A Burnable Book* and *The Invention of Fire* have come in discovering those traces for myself, and working them into a scene, a character arc, a turn of plot.

Take Southwark. It was here, at the Tabard Inn (along the current Borough High Street), that the fellowship assembled for the pilgrimage imagined in the *Canterbury Tales* by Geoffrey Chaucer, an important character in both *A Burnable Book* and *The Invention of Fire*. It was in and around these Southwark haunts, just about six centuries ago, that my novels' historical protagonist lived a good portion of his adult life. Beginning around 1377, the poet John Gower let a house and small chapel from the church of St. Mary Overie (now Southwark Cathedral), an Augustinian priory that sat in the shadow of Winchester Palace, house of the powerful bishops of Winchester. The ruins of the palace's great hall and the door to the buttery are nicely preserved just up the street from the cathedral. Gower's house was likely situated along the priory's outer walls, signaling his double orientation toward the church and the outside world.

Southwark Cathedral is a bit off the beaten path, at least for tourists. During my visits to the church, I have often been the sole person in the place experiencing it as a sightseer rather than as a parishioner or an employee. Gower's tomb sits in a recess along the north aisle, with soaring ogees over three trefoiled arches, each poised above one of the allegorical figures of Charity, Mercy, and Pity. Garishly restored in the 1950s, the tomb depicts the poet in effigy, his head on a pillow made up of his three major works of poetry.

Standing in front of Gower's tomb, leaning back against the pews, I've thought more than once about the often invisible pressures of place on the formation of literary character, particularly on those figures from the past brought to new life in historical fiction. Gower offers a wonderfully ambivalent case in point. He was a loyal and devout parishioner, by all indications, yet with a nose for iniquity that must have been sharpened by experience and by the moral geography of Southwark itself, seat of bishops and taverners, prostitutes and Austin canons, chapels and stews. Such contradictions are ripe for the speculative reconstruction of character that historical fiction allows us to pursue.

Indeed, it is in these brief placings of character that some of the most interesting work in historical fiction occurs. Think of Hilary Mantel's Thomas Cromwell, who slips with such ease in and out of his home at Austin Friars that the house becomes as much a part of the man as his limbs ("The paneling has been painted. He walks into the subdued green and golden glow").

But what if your character simply can't see the setting you create for him or her—or can't see it very well? A formidable challenge in writing from the historical viewpoint of John Gower has come in imagining and accounting for the poet's blindness. We know that Gower was blind or nearly so by the early years of Henry IV's reign (1399-1413). There are no records of the potential cause of his affliction, nor does he say anything about whether his blindness came on over a number of years or appeared suddenly at the turn of the century. I've been working on the assumption that Gower lost his vision gradually, over a long period of time. This is an unprovable hypothesis, of course, though there is an intriguing hint at the end of his *Confessio Amantis* (completed circa 1390) that the poet was already suffering from impaired vision at the time he wrote his long Middle English poem. "Myn yhen dymme" ("My eyes dim"), Gower's narrator avows, locating the visual condition among a wider catalogue of afflictions assaulting him in his old age.

Gower writes openly about the failure of his vision in his Latin works, nowhere more movingly than in his poem "Quicquid Homo Scribat" (here in R.F. Yeager's translation):

> That was the second year of King Henry IV
> When I stopped writing, because I am blind.
> My ability serves me no further, although my will does,
> But my physical agency lacks the means to write more.
> While I was able to write, I wrote very many things with zeal;
> This part clings to the world, that part clings to God.
> Nevertheless I have left to the world its vanities still to be written,
> And with a final poem I write and I go to die.

With these and other passages from Gower's work in mind, I've thought a lot about the implications of representing a visually impaired character in a genre that places so much emphasis on the historical accuracy of sights and sites. There are any number of models, of course, including Sharon Kay Penman's Rhiannon in her Plantagenets trilogy. "The blind are often hidden away from the world, as if they are a cause for shame," Rhiannon notes in a conversation with Eleanor of Aquitaine, though she has compensated for her blindness in myriad ways. More recently, in Anthony Doerr's *All the Light We Cannot See*, a blind girl's father carves a wooden replica of nearby streets and buildings as a way of helping her navigate the town—which is also, of course, the novel's setting.

In researching the treatment of blindness in Gower's day, I've learned about medieval eyeglasses, corneal surgery (!), and other technological dimensions of the subject. I've also been struck by the frequency with which medieval writers (including Gower) draw on biblical and proverbial metaphors of blindness to discuss matters of morality, faith, and the nature of sin.

Near the beginning of *The Invention of Fire*, Gower reflects on the diverse sources of beauty around him, the many sights he will miss when his eyes finally fail:

> Dusted arcs of sunlight in the vaults of St. Paul's, crimson slick of a spring lamb's offal puddled on the wharf, fine-etched ivory of a young nun's face, prickle of stars splayed on the night. Color, form, symmetry, beauty, radiance, glow. All fading now, like the half-remembered faces of the departed: my sisters, my children, my well-beloved wife. All soon enough gone, this sweet sweet world of sight.

Gower, that is, experiences medieval London through the blurred lens of his encroaching blindness, which determines in part his relationship to the novel's setting, his historical moment, even memories of his own family. For John Gower, to see the London of his day is to see a whole visual world soon to be lost. Perhaps historical fiction has a compensatory function in this respect, providing our own world with new ways of seeing pasts otherwise lost in the shadows of history.

~

BRUCE HOLSINGER is an award-winning novelist and scholar of the medieval period. His debut novel, *A Burnable Book*, won the John Hurt Fisher Prize, was named a *New York Times Book Review* Editor's Choice, and was shortlisted by the American Library Association for Best Crime Novel of 2014. His second novel, *The Invention of Fire*, received starred reviews in *Publisher's Weekly* and *Library Journal* and was named an Amazon Book of the Month for April 2015. His essays and reviews have appeared in publications including the *New York Times*, the *New York Review of Books*, *Slate*, and the *Washington Post*, and he appears regularly on NPR. A member of the faculty of the University of Virginia, he is the recipient of Guggenheim, American Council of Learned Societies and National Endowment for the Humanities fellowships. Find him online at www.bruceholsinger.com.

ANDREW HUGHES

The Convictions of John Delahunt

*T*he crux of my novel *The Convictions of John Delahunt* has been summarized as follows: On a cold December morning in 1841 Dublin, a small boy is enticed away from his mother and savagely murdered. This could be just one more death in a city riven by poverty, inequality, and political unrest, but the murder causes a public outcry. It appears the culprit—a feckless student named John Delahunt—is also an informant in the pay of the police authorities at Dublin Castle. Strangely, the young man seems neither to regret what he did, nor fear his punishment. Instead, as he awaits the hangman in his cell, John Delahunt decides to tell his story in a final, deeply unsettling statement.

I remember when I first came across John Delahunt's story: It was while researching my first book, a social history based on the inhabitants of Fitzwilliam Square, Dublin, called *Lives Less Ordinary*. One of the square's residents was Edward Pennefather, Lord Chief Justice of the Queen's Bench. He presided over the trial of Irish political leader and advocate for Catholic emancipation, Daniel O'Connell, in 1844 for conspiracy to repeal the Act of Union, which had joined Ireland with Great Britain. In *Lives Less Ordinary*, I found it was possible to retell much of Irish history through the perspectives of Fitzwilliam Square residents, by following them to political gatherings, or on to the battlefield, or in the case of Mr. Pennefather, into the courtroom.

So I set about searching for descriptions of the trial. The following, for instance, was written by Anthony Trollope: "Look at that big-headed, pig-faced fellow on the right —that's Pennefather! He's the blackest sheep of the lot—and the head of them! He's a thoroughbred Tory, and as fit to be a judge as I am to be a general."

The outcome of O'Connell's trial was never in doubt, mainly because the jury was packed with twelve Protestants. Trollope again: "Fancy a jury chosen out of all Dublin, and not one Catholic!" Charles Gavan Duffy described the Repeal leader's reaction to the guilty verdict: "O'Connell himself at that time whispered to one of the traversers that the Attorney General was moderate in only charging them with conspiracy, as those twelve gentlemen would have made no difficulty in convicting them of the murder of the Italian boy."

I paused when I came upon that passage, intrigued by the title given to the crime, the clues about the unnamed victim, and the fact that O'Connell could allude to its notoriety. Duffy added his own footnote: "The murder of the Italian boy was a mysterious crime which had recently caused a sensation in Dublin and baffled the skill of the police."

When I sought out articles relating to the murder, I first came across the names Dominico Garlibardo, Richard Cooney, and the Crown witness, John Delahunt.

Lives Less Ordinary stemmed from my fascination with the people who lived in Dublin's Georgian houses, and the fragments of history they left behind: a coat of arms hidden in a stained-glass fanlight; a letter from a young lady to her mother describing her first dinner party; a simple childhood drawing of infant brothers playing in a nursery, viewed while knowing one of their lives would end on a battlefield. The research carried out for that book provided a setting for Delahunt's story, as well as a cast of characters. Bit-part players such as Professor Lloyd, Dr. Moore, Captain Dickenson, were all, in reality, Fitzwilliam Square inhabitants.

As for Delahunt's exploits, there were any number of sources to consult: medical, court and newspaper reports, editorials and pamphlets. *The Convictions of John Delahunt* is primarily a work of fiction, especially with regards to Delahunt's character, background and family, but the set-piece events were based on real episodes: the attack on Captain Craddock, the murder of Garlibardo, and the murder of Thomas Maguire.

There were two sources that I used directly. The first was the report of a phrenologist who studied and interviewed Delahunt while he was awaiting the gallows in 1842. The doctor even made a plaster cast of Delahunt's head—who knows, that may still exist somewhere, hidden away in someone's loft. By rendering that encounter in the very first scene, I was able to establish my version of Delahunt's character. He's shown to be an object of morbid fascination, someone who is confined and condemned by Victorian society, but also as someone who can closely observe it. It was odd, but often fun, to be in Delahunt's consciousness. Whenever he was faced with a situation, I just had to imagine the most cynical, most darkly humorous response possible, and have him do that. But it was a strange head-space to inhabit, especially when dealing with his crimes and other harrowing scenes.

The second direct source was the convict's final statement. Printed in the newspapers on the morning of his execution, the confession exposed the inner workings of Dublin Castle to public scrutiny and comment. Soon after, a pamphlet appeared in the stalls of booksellers written under the alias An Informer. The pamphlet began:

> Although the public had been previously aware of the nefarious system by which informations [sic] against criminals were obtained in Dublin, they were by no means prepared for the startling disclosure of Delahunt, that the nature of the system was such as to actually tempt the informer to commit the crime, for the sole purpose of prosecuting and convicting an innocent person of it, and thus entitling himself to the blood-money.

In reality, Delahunt's evidence against Richard Cooney wasn't believed, and the murder of the Italian boy remained unsolved. Frank Thorpe, a police magistrate writing his memoirs in 1875, said: "I strongly suspect that if Delahunt really knew anything about the crime, it was owing to himself being the perpetrator." But Thorpe also wished to dispel the notion that Delahunt was in the pay of the Castle:

For a considerable time after his execution, he was reputed, especially amongst the humbler classes, to have been a police spy, and to have been in receipt of frequent subsidies from the detective office...I feel perfectly satisfied that, instead of deriving the wages of an informer or spy from the metropolitan police or from the constabulary, he never cost the public one penny beyond what sufficed for his maintenance in gaol whilst under committal for his diabolical offence, and to provide the halter which he most thoroughly deserved.

Born in Ireland, **ANDREW HUGHES** was educated at Trinity College, Dublin. It was while researching his acclaimed social history of Fitzwilliam Square—*Lives Less Ordinary: Dublin's Fitzwilliam Square, 1798-1922*—that he first came across the true story of John Delahunt, which inspired his debut novel. Andrew's second novel, *The Coroner's Daughter*, will appear in the UK in February 2017. Andrew lives in Dublin.

J. SYDNEY JONES

The Viennese Mysteries

*T*he *Third Place* is the sixth and final installment in my Viennese Mystery series, set at the turn of the 20th century and featuring private inquiries agent Advokat Karl Werthen and his partner in crime detection (and real-life father of criminology), the Austrian Hans Gross. In this series installment, Werthen and Gross investigate the murder of Herr Karl, a renowned headwaiter at one of Vienna's premier cafés. As the investigation turns up new clues, Werthen and Gross are suddenly interrupted in their work by a person they cannot refuse: They are commissioned to locate a missing letter from the Emperor to his mistress, the famous actress Katharina Schratt. Emperor Franz Josef is desperate for the letter not to fall into the wrong hands, for it contains a damning secret. As the intrepid investigators press on with this new investigation, they soon discover that there has also been an attempt to assassinate the emperor. Eventually, Werthen and Gross realize that the case of the murdered headwaiter and the continuing plot to kill the emperor are connected, and they now face their most challenging and dangerous investigation yet.

This novel takes its title from the Viennese saying, *First is home, next comes work, and then the third place is the coffeehouse.* In fact, much of the inspiration for the writing of this book comes from the Viennese coffeehouse and its history and legends. Dialogue in the book describes the putative origins of the city's first coffeehouse. Vienna was besieged by the Ottoman Empire for two months in mid-1683. After the Turks were routed on September 12, 1683, by a relieving force of 120,000 Germans and Poles, the spoils were handed out all around. The Turks had taken most of their treasury with them, but among other things left behind were sacks and sacks full of coffee beans. The Viennese had yet to discover the joys of coffee; the story—probably mostly myth—goes that a loyal Polish trader named Kolschitzky was rewarded for his spying services during the Turkish siege of Vienna by making off with bags of coffee beans found in the camp of the vanquished Turks. Kolschitzky knew of the wonderful beverage from his time in Constantinople, and he agreed to take these "useless beans" as a further reward for his service to Vienna. He proceeded to open Vienna's first coffeehouse, At the Sign of the Blue Bottle, and started what has become a Viennese institution.

For those of you who love to ponder Lorenz's "butterfly theory" or play "six degrees of separation," the world of Vienna 1900 is no stranger. Going forward or backward in time, you're pretty likely to hit on a link in *fin de siècle* Vienna if you're dealing with someone in the arts, literature, science, or world affairs. From Freud to Mahler, Klimt, and Hitler, the city was an amazing cauldron of cultural innovation (and, yes, in Hitler's case, destruction) around the turn of the previous century—and you would encounter most if not all of these figures at Vienna's coffeehouses.

At the epicenter of it all was the young polymath Karl Kraus, cultural critic, grammar policeman, and word maven of Vienna 1900. Kraus, a frail-looking man, beavered away for over three decades, single-handedly publishing his magazine, *Die Fackel (The Torch)*. In this journal he took on the hypocrisies of the day, stood up to the rich and the powerful when need be, fought crime and societal stupidity, and generally pissed off everybody. The ultimate aphorist, Kraus termed Vienna 1900 a "laboratory for world destruction."

Kraus has served as a source of information for Werthen several times in my series. In my novel *Requiem in Vienna*, I describe him thusly: "A slight man with a curly head of hair and tiny oval wire-rim glasses that reflected the overhead lights, Kraus dressed like a banker. One of nine children of a Bohemian Jew who had made his money from paper bags, Kraus lived on a family allowance that allowed him to poke fun at everyone in the pages of his journal."

Kraus, frankly, did not care who he angered. And sometimes he paid the price for his outspoken views. Once part of the *Jung Wien* group of writers, including, among others, Arthur Schnitzler—whom Freud termed his double—and the young Felix Salten—later author of *Bambi*—Kraus soon turned against them. In a famous article, he ridiculed the group's coffee-house culture and earned what we now call a bitch slap from Salten at the Café Central for his words. On another occasion, he took a punch on the nose from an irate cabaret performer who did not care for Kraus's reviews.

Kraus was most definitely a man of contradictions, and no one ever said he was likable. Something of the H.L. Mencken of Vienna, Kraus enjoyed a turn of phrase, enjoyed shocking people. But most of all he enjoyed being at the center of the rippling pool of 1900 Vienna's artists and intellectuals. He was the ultimate filter of gossip in fin de siècle Vienna; he knew where all the bodies were buried.

Kraus was also a major celebrity in his day. "I am already so popular that anyone who vilifies me becomes more popular than I am," he liked to say. Besides the regular publication of his journal, Kraus was also a performer. Again from *Requiem in Vienna*:

> Despite his slightness of bearing, Kraus had a fine speaking voice. He had tried for a career as an actor as a younger man, but stage fright had intervened. He was said to be experimenting with a new form of entertainment, however, much like the American Mark Twain and his famous one-person shows. At fashionable salons, Kraus was already entertaining the *cognoscenti* with his interpretations of Shakespeare and with readings from his own writings. Another of his aphorisms Werthen had heard: "When I read, it is not acted literature; but what I write is written acting."

And oh my, but he makes one hell of a fictional character. So acerbic, so full of self-contradictions, so full of himself. I am not sure I would have liked to sit down over a cup of coffee or glass of wine with the man—nor he with me, I am sure—but anybody who could quip that "psychoanalysis is that disease of which it purports to be the cure" would have been worth knowing.

J. SYDNEY JONES is the author of numerous books of fiction and nonfiction, including the novels of the critically acclaimed Viennese Mystery series: *The Empty Mirror, Requiem in Vienna, The Silence, The Keeper of Hands, A Matter of Breeding* and *The Third Place.* He lived for many years in Vienna and has written several other books about the city, including the narrative history *Hitler in Vienna: 1907-1913*, the popular walking guide *Viennawalks*, and the thriller *Time of the Wolf.* Jones is also the author of the stand-alone thrillers *Ruin Value: A Mystery of the Third Reich* (2013), *The German Agent* (2014), and *Basic Law* (2015). He has lived and worked as a correspondent and freelance writer in Paris, Florence, Molyvos, and Donegal, and currently resides with his wife and son on the coast of central California. Visit him at www.jsydneyjones.com.

M.R.C. KASASIAN

The Gower Street Detective Books

or nearly five years, way back in the 1970s, I studied Dentistry at University College Hospital, London, and for most of that time I lived in the Medical School hostel on Gower Street. This consisted of nine Victorian terraced houses knocked into one but still retaining their individuality, each having a staircase rising four lofty stories. I lived in number 125, the old black front door sealed but still bearing the original brass lion's-head knocker. My room was in the basement at the front, looking into the moat that separated it from the pavement and with a view of the constant stream of pedestrians' feet hurrying about their business.

In one corner of the room was a substantial cupboard built into a recess with a few shelves above a broken wooden rail. It was when I was standing in the cupboard trying to mend that rail that I had an itch in my foot and, bending to scratch it, noticed that a board in the base had tipped upwards at one end. Stepping back, I found that the other boards lifted too and that beneath them was a cavity in which had been placed a long wooden box, thick with dust and mold. My curiosity aroused, I hauled it—with considerable difficulty, for it was extremely heavy—out and onto the floor. The wood was so rotten that it was breaking up under its own weight to reveal a grey surface underneath. Lifting the hinged lid, I realized that the box was lined in asbestos (this was before we had much idea of the perils of such a material) and packed with red leather- covered books, the top left of one embossed in gold letters *Journal 1882*. I took the book out and opened the cover to find the first page dated Sunday, January 1st, and, beneath the date, four paragraphs of neat little writing in pencil. *A cold start to the year and wet. Spent most of the day attempting to make some sense of poor Papa's accounts. They are such a muddle I hardly know where to begin but I am determined put my affairs in order this year.*

There followed a few sentences about bonds and shares and I was rapidly losing interest until a line near the end caught my eye. *A frugal supper in the snug watching the sun set over Ashurst Beacon.*

I flicked through a few pages and it was soon apparent that the diarist was writing from The Grange, a house I had often passed on walks to admire the very same view at the top of Parbold Hill in the village where I had grown up.

I skimmed through. There was more talk of financial problems, solicitors, visiting a friend with the unlikely name of Maudy Glass, and taking a train from Parbold to Wigan to London on the very route I had travelled the best part of a century later.

There was some chatter about sharing cigarettes and gin with a slightly disreputable teacher's wife called Harriet Fitzpatrick and realizing that Mr. Sidney Grice (the writer's godfather, with whom she was going to live) was a famous private detective. The writer's name, it transpired, was March Middleton.

I read on and, almost immediately March was embroiled in investigating the murder of a young woman in the East End. She and her guardian set off to examine the victim's body and then:

It occurs to me that much that am I writing of is highly confidential and that it might be prudent to use my father's code system to protect my account from prying eyes.

And there it began, a meaningless (to me) jumble of numbers separated by commas and broken into small groups of differing lengths by spaces.

At first I nearly tossed the book aside, but I was intrigued. I had played with codes as a child. I could have a go at cracking this one. After a fruitless hour or so I went to the pub.

In the Duke of Wellington pub, which was down a side road off Gower Street, I treated myself to a half-pint of bitter, which was all I could afford and sat at the bar with the book and a paper and pencil. Some of the numbers seemed too big to represent the letters of the alphabet, going well over 100.

"It appears to be a straight number-for-letter transposition," a voice said, and I twisted my neck to see a dark-haired man in an immaculately tailored three-piece pinstripe suit peering over my shoulder.

"I thought of that," I told him, slightly affronted at his presumptuousness. "But I can't see any pattern to it."

"May I?" The stranger leafed through a few pages. "It's a sort of hobby of mine."

We chatted a bit more, and it was clear that he knew a great deal more about the subject than I did, and before I knew it, I had agreed to lend him the journal over the weekend.

"You'll be alright with Mr. Smith," Tom, the barman told me. "He's a regular here and a real gent."

And, true to his word, Mr. Smith returned on the Monday evening, carrying a black attaché case.

"Daniel, Chapter 4: Verse 37," he announced, placing the journal on the bar and a typed sheet of paper on top reading in double-spaced lines, "NOW I NEBUCHADNEZZAR PRAISE AND EXTOL AND HONOR THE KING OF HEAVEN, ALL WHOSE WORKS *ARE* TRUTH, AND HIS WAYS JUDGMENT: AND THOSE THAT WALK IN PRIDE HE IS ABLE TO ABASE."

"It's quite simple," he explained. "You just need a sentence containing all the letters of the alphabet, and the Victorians did love their Bible quotes."

Underneath each letter he had printed a number, 1 to 137.

'The only letter that's missing is Q. So she gives that the number 138.'

"So N is 1," I began but Mr. Smith corrected me patiently.

"Only the first time she uses it. The second time she picks N's second appearance so it becomes number 5."

"So A can be..." I counted along. "Numbers 11, 17, 21 and so on."

"Exactly," he agreed.

"But how on earth did you work that out?"

"Had a bit of help from the office computer," he confessed. "I've done a sample paragraph for you. After that you're on your own."

And I saw that on the back of the page he had written: *I saw now what Mrs. Dillinger meant by "so much blood." The walls and furniture were splattered with it, dried and blackened and there was a coagulated puddle with dozens of bootprints all over the uncarpeted floor.*

There followed March Middleton's description of the scene of the murder of Sarah Ashby, which she used in her account of what was to be known as *The Mangle Street Murders*.

I thanked Mr. Smith and was financially relieved when he turned down my offer to buy him a drink. He came back to Duke of Wellington often but it was soon obvious that he had no interest in me other than the intellectual challenge I had set him. He did not even care what the rest of the diaries said, and with the pressure of exams and later the commitments of General Practice and family life, it was many years before I had the leisure time to translate them in full. There were 32 volumes in all, and they had been placed in their asbestos hiding place in the basement in 1940 to protect them during the Blitz.

About six months later I spotted Mr. Smith across the road in Gower Street at the Euston Road end, smartly attired as always and carrying his attaché case and a rolled umbrella. I raised my hand in greeting, but he was hurrying away through the side door of a nondescript 1960s building and I never saw him again.

It was only after I quit dentistry and gave the journals the attention they deserved that I discovered that some of them had been published but were now long out of print and that many of the adventures—*The Sign of the Fourteen*, for example—had been shamelessly plagiarized by the alleged creator of Sherlock Holmes, Sir Arthur Conan Doyle, who had been forced to settle with March Middleton out of court to save himself from public humiliation and bankruptcy.

I did a little research into the history of Gower Street. Wikipedia was an obvious starting point and there was a brief statement at the end of the article.

"From 1976 until 1995 the headquarters of MI5 were an anonymous grey office block at 140 Gower Street, adjacent to the Euston Road. The site has since been redeveloped."

And so it appears that we have Her Majesty's Secret Service to thank for translating the lost journals of March Middleton and resurrecting her accounts of her wonderful adventures with Mr. Sidney Grice, the ingenious, albeit curmudgeonly, Gower Street detective.

~

M. R. C. KASASIAN is the author of the Gower Street Detective Books: *The Mangle Street Murders, The Curse of the House of Foskett, Death Descends on Saturn Villa,* and *The Secrets of Gaslight Lane.* He lives with his wife in England. Follow him on Twitter at @MRCKASASIAN.

PHILIP KAZAN

~

The Painter of Souls

I first saw the paintings of Fra Filippo Lippi, the subject/
hero/antihero of my new novel, *The Painter of Souls*, on a
school trip to Florence. My parents had scraped together their last pennies and sent me off with the History of Art class.
I wasn't even studying History of Art, but my artist mother thought
it would be good for me and it was.

Of course, we spent hours in the Uffizi Gallery, where my 15-year-
old self was alternately ravished by the paintings and racked with
boredom, desperate to peel off and wander the noisy streets outside,
to look at the fashions, to listen to the music of Italian being spoken;
above all, to gaze at the beautiful women.

To a teenager from the wilds of Devon—our house had only got
electricity six years earlier, and we only had one grainy channel on
our black-and-white TV—these women were creatures from another
world. I marveled at them, not as objects of earthly desire but as
angels. Which was just as well: spotty, trying to smoke my Nazionale

cigarettes with the *sprezzatura*—nonchalance—of the Italian *ragazzi* and failing miserably, I knew perfectly well that I didn't have a chance. *Sprezzatura* is the art of making something very difficult—the impeccable street style of Italians being an excellent example—look effortless. But, back then, I was taking something relatively easy and making it look virtually impossible. No *sprezzatura* for me.

So I let myself surrender to pure, unalloyed wonder. The whole place was wonderful. The smells billowing from restaurants—grilling meat, hot olive oil, roasting coffee; the heavy golden light in the palms and olive trees; an orange tree gilded with fruit in the cloister of San Lorenzo. Michelangelo's captives in the Academia. Silk ties in the window of Pucci on Via Tornabuoni. The clack of high heels on flagstones. Masaccio's Holy Trinity and the Brancacci Chapel. San Marco, where the luminous glories of Fra Angelico's paintings lead you to Savonarola's cell and the Bonfire of the Vanities. Drinking *vin santo* in a café under the scornful eyes of the locals—if only I could go back in time and order a grappa instead.

That week changed me forever: the outside got in. I learned to live with my senses wide open. I found the ecstasy of the everyday. What a gift. When I got back to Devon I found I'd taken some of it back with me. What I remembered, most of all, were the paintings of the early 15th century: Botticelli, of course. Masaccio. Ghirlandaio and Fra Angelico. But it was Fra Filippo Lippi who really stuck with me. His faces most of all. They seemed to glow with a pure inner light, as though the artist had captured what I had been feeling there in Florence: the beauty that comes when you open yourself up to the beauty of the world.

Yes, the world is beautiful to a teenager on a safe, curated school outing. The world of Fra Filippo, though, was anything but safe. He had spent his childhood as an orphan on the streets of Oltrarno, entered the Friary of Santa Maria del Carmine at 14, lived the life of a professional artist when the profession could literally be cut-throat. He was always short of money—his money troubles led him to the torture chambers of the Signoria. We glean these facts from a few of his letters that survive, from the ledgers of the Carmine and the official record of his legal woes, and almost nothing else. He ended up at the very pinnacle of his trade but his life was never easy and at times extremely hard. His Florence wasn't anything like the one I discovered. And yet he painted such beauty.

Fra Filippo painted himself into his sublime *Coronation of the Virgin*, which was commissioned by the church of Sant'Ambrogio. His eyes are heavy with lack of sleep and he hasn't shaved for a couple of days. Chin propped on a hand—am I imagining paint under the fingernails?—he is watching us as we stare at his work. He's watching us gaze at the Virgin, at the saints and angels, but I can't help thinking, most of all at the dazzlingly beautiful young woman who is also looking out of the painting at us. His gaze, hers, ours. There is a triangle of complicity here, a moment where we are observed as we ourselves observe.

This is an altarpiece, painted for the nuns of Sant'Ambrogio to worship (which explains the slight foreshortening of the figures in the foreground: they were intended to be seen from below, by kneeling devotees). The young woman is Mary Magdalen, an object of their worship. But the Magdalen was also a woman of the world. Her gaze is knowing in many dimensions. She meets our eyes knowing very well that we find her beautiful. She is aware of our desire as well as our devotion. Fra Filippo knows it too. Somewhere inside this trinity, perhaps, is a clue to understanding where his mastery of human beauty comes from. He has allowed the churchgoers of Florence to be pious devotees and, simultaneously, admiring *ragazzi*. He makes sure we're getting the whole picture, leaning on his hand, his work done. Friar and *ragazzo*.

Is that Fra Filippo's great gift? That he lets us be what we want, in front of his paintings? Connoisseurs of fleshly beauty can feast their eyes on women and men who, despite their seeming perfection, aren't ideals or cyphers but real people who were walking the streets of Florence in the 1440s, just as they are today. And the devoted can find transcendence shining through the paint with tangible power. Atheists like me can feel it too. Filippo, I feel sure, intended both things, because he had both impulses within him, and gave them equal freedom in his art—and, plainly, his life. Perhaps that's what I learned, spotty, 15 and unsupervised: to let both sides, heaven and earth, find their balance.

If I did, I didn't realize it straight away. I lit another Nazionale and wandered onto the Ponte Vecchio, or through the lanes between the Duomo and the Piazza Signoria, and let it all soak in.

⁓

PHILIP KAZAN is the pseudonym of British author Pip-Vaughan Hughes, the author of the four Brother Petroc novels set in the 13th century. *The Painter of Souls* is his first book to be published in the US.

JENNIFER KINCHELOE

The Secret Life of Anna Blanc

*I*n 1910, Alice Stebbins Wells became the first female cop in Los Angeles. Brilliant, brave, and politic, she held her own with the boys. No, she outshone them. I stumbled across a story about her life—just a couple of paragraphs, because very little is written about her. It sparked my imagination and led me to write my novel *The Secret Life of Anna Blanc*.

I had intended to write a sensible, experienced, civic-minded character, like Alice Stebbins Wells. Instead, my protagonist came tumbling out as a cross between Sherlock Holmes and Scarlett O'Hara.

I couldn't help it. The character wrote herself.

In my book, socialite Anna Blanc buys off her chaperone and uses an alias to secretly get a job as a matron with the Los Angeles Police Department (LAPD). She uncovers a string of brothel murders that the cops are unwilling to investigate. Anna must solve the crimes while maintaining her secret identity.

If the police find out, she's fired. If her father finds out, he'll disown her. If her fiancé finds out, he'll call off the engagement *and* the money he's pouring into her father's collapsing bank.

Writing this book was a stretch for me. I knew nothing about the Progressive Era. I had never written historical fiction. Actually, I had never written a novel.

Years of research awaited me, and over 150 drafts of what would become *The Secret Life of Anna Blanc*.

Because men wrote history and women are mostly left out, my research focused on things written *during* the early 1900s, not just books written *about* them. I read women's memoirs, novels written by women, advice books for brides and single women, a female humorist's tips on dealing with men, cookbooks, books on how to do laundry, an etiquette manual, the ladies' section of the newspaper, advertisements, love song lyrics, suffrage speeches, court transcripts, want ads, and newspaper stories about women and women's organizations. I found a historian who studied early-20th-century prostitution in Los Angeles and obtained her dissertation on microfiche from the library.

I also read about men and their world: sermons, a coroner's manual, eyewitness accounts, a police department's annual report, and lots and lots of newspaper articles about the antics of the LAPD and their quarry.

Period photographs helped me to flesh out the details, to provide color and texture to the novel. I collected over 30,000 of them, all still viewable on my Pinterest page.

I continued to research the book until it was typeset for printing.

Once I had a handle on the period, I had to displace real history to make room for my story. I chose to fictionalize everyone. In 1907, the LAPD employed two police matrons, Alice Stebbins Wells and Aletha Gilbert. I erased them from history, replacing them with Anna Blanc and a second fictional character, Matron Clemens (who really is modeled after Alice Stebbins Wells).

I'm going to be perfectly frank here. Historically, Anna Blanc's character felt like a leap. Police matrons were required to be older, sober-minded women who had been married and had a zeal for lost souls. They were typically from the middle class. But that's not the protagonist who called to me. The one that flowed out of my fingertips was naïve, spoiled, beautiful, and super rich.

There is a tension when you write historical fiction. How much liberty can you take for the sake of the story? I couldn't hold true to the requirements for LAPD matrons and write this particular book. That bothered me. But the character made sense in my story, and I had a good rationale for how she got where she got, so I finished the novel hoping no one would call me on it.

Then something marvelous happened. After the book was written, I stumbled across a newly published biography about a real-life police matron, Fanny Bixby (later Fanny Bixby Spenser), who was young, beautiful, single, and the daughter of one of the richest men in California. She became a matron in Long Beach in 1908 when she was still in her twenties. Like Anna Blanc, Fanny carried a gun. More than once, she took a beating. Like my fictional character, high society and Fanny's family frowned upon her law enforcement endeavors. Suddenly, my Anna Blanc seemed more plausible.

It reminded me that the actual past (that is, all of the things that really happened in the great, wide world) is far broader than my conception of history (that is, a story full of holes, constructed primarily by white men). In the real past, rules were broken. Mores were occasionally thrown out the window. Unlikely characters did extraordinary things. Women especially transcended their role in society. Just because we don't know something happened doesn't mean it couldn't have happened—or didn't.

This discovery taught me to trust my instincts. Because history is fraught with gaps, we have to use our imaginations to make it come alive. Research only goes so far. We fill in the holes with story. And most of the time, our fiction is no stranger than the truth.

When I finished *The Secret Life of Anna Blanc*, I contacted the Los Angeles historian I've mentioned, who specialized in prostitution in the early 20th century. I begged her to read the book and review it for accuracy. Although I was a total stranger, she graciously agreed.

She gave the novel the big thumbs up, and said it made her smile.

∼

JENNIFER KINCHELOE is a research scientist turned writer of historical fiction. She earned a Masters degree in Public Health from Loma Linda University and a Ph.D. in Health Services from UCLA. She adores kickboxing, yoga, and developing complex statistical models. She was on the faculty at UCLA, where she spent 11 years conducting research to inform health policy. She currently lives in Denver, Colorado, with her husband and two children. *The Secret Life of Anna Blanc* is her first novel. For more information, visit her website at www.jenniferkincheloe.com and her Pinterest page (where thousands of images related to the book and its time period can be found) at www.pinterest.com/jrobin66.

DERYN LAKE

~

The John Rawlings Mysteries

As all my readers will know, John Rawlings really lived. He was an apothecary, dwelling in London, who applied to be made Free of the Worshipful Society of Apothecaries on 22nd August, 1754, finally achieving his freedom on 13th March, 1755. His friend John Fielding (the Blind Beak) was a historical character too.

In 1983, about 30 years ago, I was approached by Canada Dry to try to discover the origins of H.D. Rawlings Ltd., a label for soda and tonic waters that they had inherited due to various take-overs. They had a suspicion that Rawlings was older than its rival, Schweppes, because of some correspondence that they had acquired. These letters were signed by Henry Doo Rawlings and dated 1870. The address given was 2, Nassau Street, Soho, with the inscription beneath stating, "Trading at these premises for over 100 years." If this information was true it meant that Rawlings was founded circa 1770, whereas Jacob Schweppe started his business in 1783.

Just an aside about Henry Doo Rawlings. In the reign of Queen Victoria the entire Rawlings empire eventually devolved onto one widow, Sarah, already in her fifties. She had working for her a young clerk called Henry Doo, who, quite honestly, she must have fancied enormously. She proposed to him, offering him control of the business, provided that he changed his name to Rawlings. He readily agreed, they were married, and Henry Doo became the president of the company.

You have probably guessed that 1983 was an important date because Schweppes would then, with no challengers, be able to celebrate two hundred years of trading. So, having duly been shown Henry Doo's correspondence, I was given two weeks not only to find the founder of the firm but to prove that H.D. Rawlings Ltd. was indeed older that its rival.

Strangely, I found him on the first day of looking but didn't realize it. There, in *Pigot's Street Directory* for 1764, was listed a John Rawlings, Apothecary. I'm afraid I didn't make the connection and passed him by.

Eventually, after going up a great many blind alleys, I went to the Guildhall in London to look up the records of the Worshipful Society of Brewers and also the Worshipful Society of Apothecaries. I shall never forget the thrill of resting my hand— contained in a white glove, of course—on the signature of Richard Whittington, who presided over the Society of Brewers. History came utterly alive to me and I just sat transfixed—mesmerized, in fact. After all the centuries that signature was as bold and strong as when the famous man actually penned it.

To return to John Rawlings. In the records of the Worshipful
Society of Apothecaries I found that a John Rawlings,

> a foreign apothecary [*this means that he was apprenticed
> outside the City of London*] attended the Court and
> desired to be admitted to his Freedom of the Company
> by Redemption on the terms mentioned in the Court of
> Assistants of 22nd August last but not withstanding the
> Order of this Court of Assistants of the 5th December last
> whereby the Fine [*which means fee*] for admitting Foreign
> Apothecaries was increased, he having attended at the Hall
> to take up his Freedom on the Private Court Day in August
> last but the Court was just broke up and he was prevented
> by business attending again before the 5th December last,
> which being taken into consideration. Ordered that on his
> paying a fine of £7.lO.Od. to the Garden [*the Chelsea Physic
> Garden*] and Fees and passing an Examination he be made
> Free of the Company by Redemption. He paid the Fine.

Still I could not prove that this was the John Rawlings I was
looking for. So on the penultimate day of my search I returned to
the Guildhall and looked at the Society's records once more. And
there it was, missed by me the first time I had examined them. John
had given his address when he was made free. It was Number 2,
Nassau Street, Soho.

So there he was, the link had been made. If John had become a
fully-fledged apothecary in 1755 and had started experimenting
with water soon after, his company was definitely older than Jacob
Schweppe's.

Canada Dry based a TV commercial on my findings. The late
great Arthur Lowe was seen in full 18th-century costume walking

up a long red carpet towards a pair of thrones on which sat a king and queen. He was carrying a tray of tonic waters and as the camera came into close-up he turned to it and said, "Sshh! We knew how before you- know-who." I thought it very clever.

Having presented my case to Canada Dry—who were delighted with the findings —I put my file away and forgot about it. Then, as some of you may be aware, there occurred a terrific downturn in the market for historical novels. It started, as all these things do, across the Atlantic in America, and Britain, inevitably, followed suit. I was in a state, envisaging my livelihood flying out of the window. Then I had a chat with an old friend of mine who had been in publishing for years, and he advised me to turn my attention towards crime.

I deliberated and then, like a flash, I remembered John Rawlings and started to investigate the times in which he lived. And who should I find but the Blind Beak, John Fielding himself, alive at the same time and Principal Magistrate. I had my detective and *Death in the Dark Walk* was born.

The rest, as they say, is history. Fifteen more novels later—the most recent brings him to Boston, where he happens upon a peculiar sort of tea party—I've come to love my fictional John Rawlings, and I'm pleased that readers seem to love him too.

DERYN LAKE is the pseudonym of well-known historical novelist Dinah Lampitt. Her historical mystery series featuring Apothecary John Rawlings now numbers 16 titles. She also writes a contemporary mystery series featuring the Reverend Nick Lawrence; like the John Rawlings books, the Nick Lawrence books—The *Mills of God, Dead on Cue* and *The Moonlit Door*— are published by Severn House. She lives near Hastings in East Sussex in the UK. Find out more about the author and her books at www.derynlake.com.

DEBORAH LAWRENSON

~

300 Days of Sun and Other Works

*T*hough readers have often commented on my novels' sense of place, I never set out to write novels that were particu-larly known for that. I set out to write stories that rang true and that transported the reader into another place and time, drawn into authentic surroundings, experiencing what my characters were seeing and hearing, smelling and tasting.

As Simone de Beauvoir tells us in her autobiographical *Force of Circumstance:* "I do not mention the colour of the sky, the taste of a fruit, out of self-indulgence....Not only do [these details] allow us to apprehend a period and a person in flesh and blood, but by their non-significance they are the very touch of truth in a true story."

It's an important insight. How do you make a setting of a novel seem truthful and vivid to someone else? One way is to remind them of what they already know, even if that's subconsciously. In fact, stirring subconscious memories is a crucial part of it. It is an appeal to the senses, reminding readers of the time they visited the South of France, or Italy, or Greece, calling on dormant memories. We are all fascinated by reading what others think about places we know well, feeling that familiarity, wanting our own experiences to be reflected and yet looking beneath the surface for new insights too.

The obvious way to appeal to readers who have never been to these places is to write visually, to describe what the place looks like. But underneath that, you have to try to capture the essence of a setting.

In my novel *The Lantern*, set in Provence, the sense of place is strengthened by the scents of the landscape. The interesting thing about lavender and other aromas is that part of the brain seems to be able to recreate the smell in the imagination. Many people have written to tell me that while they were reading the book they felt they could almost smell the lavender. I think that's because when we think of lavender, we not only instinctively call on our memory of its distinct perfume, but we see it, either in bunches of dried stems, or waves of purple fields, or distilled in a cologne bottle. Our own experiences and memories do much of the writer's work.

A description of wild thyme releasing its scent in the heat will bring the scrubby hillsides of *garrigue* to the mind's eye. A café setting will be enhanced by the mention of the rich aroma of continental coffee. Cigarette smoke inside is now strictly for historical sections! As Simone de Beauvoir says, it's the small details that bring a scene to life, making the story seem real.

Scents and perfumes came into their own—along with the character of Marthe, the blind *parfumière*—in the central novella of my next novel, *The Sea Garden*. The story is told across three separate but carefully linked novellas.

In atmosphere, the three novellas are sharply defined. The first, *The Sea Garden*, is set in the near present on the island of Porquerolles. It's all color and blossoming trees, plants and turquoise sea. But there's a dreamy quality about it too, almost hyper-real, the explanation for which becomes clear by the end of the book. The third novella, *A Shadow Life*, is set in a bomb-blasted London, during the Second World War. It's monochrome: darkness and moonlight and unease. The rare splashes of color are intended to stand out and highlight links to the other sections.

In the middle novella, *The Lavender Field*, there's a real challenge. I had to imagine what Marthe's life might have been like in Manosque in the 1930s. She is apprenticed to a small factory that makes soaps and *eau de toilette* from local ingredients, as many local lavender distilleries still do today. There was another challenge to writing about Marthe, and that was that she lost her sight as a child. And I write from her point of view. However, I discovered that writing non-visually was not only possible, but recalled the landscape in a very intense way—by sound, by smell and taste and touch, using all the senses except the visual sense. I had to focus on the way that lyrical prose can convey subtle messages and layers of meaning.

The seeds of my new novel *300 Days of Sun* were sown when I went to Faro, in southern Portugal, to accompany my 17-year-old daughter. She wanted to apply to study Spanish and Portuguese at university and had enrolled in a two-week Portuguese language course in the town.

While she got to grips with a new language, I wandered around the old town with my notebook and camera, and let my imagination flow. The following observations appear as Joanna's experiences in the novel.

> My first few days in the country, I was astonished by how many Russian tourists there were here, chattering in the shops and streets. Then I realized: to the uninitiated, Portuguese sounds like Russian. The language is nothing like the soft singsong of Spanish or Italian. The sounds shush and slip around like the shining, sliding cobblestones under your feet.
>
> The temperature was climbing. The air was heavy with orange dust from the Sahara that fell like a sprinkling of paprika powder over the town's white sills and ledges. I walked down to the ferry, needing to get out over water to catch some fresh wind. As the boat ploughed through green salt marshes, I did breathe more easily.

Joanna is a journalist who travels to Faro looking for breathing space; she meets Nathan, a charismatic younger man who challenges her expectations and leads her to a dark story of past consequences. Superficially, these are simple impressions of a place —a real place. But on closer examination, several recurrent themes of the book are embedded: the mistaken impressions; the unstable ground; the entrapping heat of the South; the difficulty, despite Joanna's hopes, of finding a breathing space; the constant movement and crossing of borders.

The story emerged from my researches into the fascinating years of the Second World War, when Portugal, as a neutral country, was a cauldron of intrigue, spies, enemies, opportunists, and double-dealers, especially around Lisbon. Since then, the dramatic, rocky Algarve coast has become known as a wonderful, friendly place to spend time in the sun—three hundred days of it a year—but there have been some dark events there too: in particular, cases of child abduction, including one notorious one.

In the writing, this novel took on a thriller-ish quality, and I found the lush and atmospheric sense of place seemed to heighten the tension: these events should not be happening in a sunny, supposedly carefree place. I looked to two of my favorite romantic suspense writers for inspiration—Mary Stewart and Daphne du Maurier, who both knew how to combine an exciting story with an evocative setting—and went with the flow.

DEBORAH LAWRENSON spent her childhood moving around the world with diplomatic service parents, from Kuwait to China, Belgium, Luxembourg and Singapore. She read English literature at Cambridge University and worked as a journalist in London. Many of her novels are set in and around the Mediterranean Sea. *The Lantern* was published to critical acclaim in the US, chosen for Channel 4's The TV Book Club Summer Reads in the UK, and shortlisted for Romantic Novel of the Year 2012. She divides her time between rural Kent and a crumbling hamlet in Provence, the atmospheric setting for *The Lantern*. Her latest novel is *300 Days of Sun*. Find her online at www.deborah-lawrenson.co.uk.

GENE LEE

~

Men Without Hate

*I*n the fall of 2004 the coast of Florida where I live was ravaged by back-to-back hurricanes. Three weeks apart, both of these storms made landfall in almost the exact same place, wreaking intensive damage in their paths. In the aftermath of the storms, while waiting for the power and some semblance of a normal life to return, I began writing what turned out to be a novella about the terrible Labor Day hurricane of 1935. My grandfather, two of his brothers, and my uncle, then 14, aboard my grandfather's boat on a weekend fishing excursion, were trapped in that storm. Presumed dead, a week and a half later they were spotted cruising up the New River to my grandfather's home in Ft. Lauderdale, the boat battered and torn, the men not faring much better—but alive.

In between making repairs to my house and picking up the other pieces after our own hurricanes, I worked on the story, completing it in December of that year. The fictionalized adventures of my grandfather's crew in the storm made for a good story, I was happy with what I had done, and I thought that was the end of it. But a few months into the following year it occurred to me that though I might be done with that particular tale, two of the characters—the father and son I had called John and Hilton Raines—were not done with me.

With the idea of a possible novel germinating in my head I wrote a story about John Raines's beginnings as a lawyer in the little town of Fort Lauderdale back in the 1920s, a lawyer whose first client was the notorious local outlaw John Ashley. I followed this with a story about Hilton Raines in boot camp before World War II. In this story Hilton signs up for the artillery in honor of his grandfather Lewis, who had been in Lee's artillery at Gettysburg. When I was finished with this tale, damned if Lewis Raines too didn't begin to occupy space in my head!

Thus began a journey in writing that lasted for the next seven years. Drawing on family history—faithfully kept by my mother, and when she passed on, my sister—as well as what I had learned over many years of studying the War Between the States, I put down what happened to Lewis at Gettysburg and thereafter. Originally I believed his would be a simple tale—one of battle and bravery and loss, all taking place on one awful day, July 3rd, 1863, remembered for Pickett's Charge. I should have known better. There will always be more to a story, if the one writing it is willing to listen, and feel, and go with the words flowing through his or her head.

In the end Lewis required three sections, all of which make up Book One of the novel I eventually called *Men Without Hate*. The first section deals with the horror of war, the second with the horrors of the Reconstruction, and the third with Lewis finding love, making a home for himself, and finally being able to recover from all that he had been through, physically, mentality, and emotionally.

Book Two is devoted to John Raines, Lewis's son, and his humble beginnings on the hardscrabble tobacco farm his father and two brothers struggle to make a living from. It's a short book, by far the shortest in the novel, but tells of a cataclysmic event that takes place one hot August day in the tobacco fields, when what should have been just another day in the life of a 12-year-old boy turns into something much more.

Book Three is Hilton's story. And here the arc of the novel, I hope, comes full circle, revealing the full scope of war and what it can do to two separate men, related by family perhaps but each of a totally different makeup.

For if Lewis is a survivor, his grandson Hilton most certainly is not. Crippled with malaria and "battle fatigue" (what today is known as PTSD), Hilton returns from war to a world that is not the one he left. His book was the hardest for me to write. Using the letters my uncle wrote home to his parents and fiancée during his time of duty in the Philippines during World War II as starting points, I wanted to put down the full range of horror and realization that comes to the fictional Hilton. War is hell, as General Sherman so famously said; in the novel, what Hilton found during and after the battle for Manila certainly proved that to be true.

At first I was leery of putting Hilton's story on paper, concerned about what my family might think. Yet I couldn't not write it. From reading my uncle's letters I began to know a man I never knew during his lifetime. While I was growing up, neither my mother nor grand-parents ever really spoke of him. It was only much later, when I had a family of my own, that my mother began to talk of her brother. Of how it was having him in her life. Of how hard it was to lose him.

I invested 10 years of my life into *Men Without Hate*. Some of that time was filled with good days with pen and paper. Some was a struggle. It took several starts and stops, the work put away after completing a section so that I could deal with other stories that came to me. But after two drafts, both very different from each other (courtesy of my diligent and wise editor), in January of 2012 the book was done to our mutual satisfaction.

Today I am able to tell myself that I did well. As much as I worried it would not be the case, I succeeded in what I set out to do: tell a story of certain men's lives, the good and the bad and the very bad, in a way that does them proud and, I hope, pleases the reader too.

Born and raised in Florida, **GENE LEE** currently lives in Indian River County. His plans to become a lawyer were derailed when at the age of 13, inspired by Ernest Hemingway and James Joyce, he began writing stories. After many years of writing and publishing his poetry in literary journals, Gene returned to his first love, fiction. Find out more about Gene and *Men Without Hate* at www.geneleeauthor.com.

JOAN LENNON

~

Silver Skin

*H*ere, Joan Lennon (below, "JL") interviews herself (below, "Joanlennon") on her novel *Silver Skin*.

JL: And what would you like me to call you?

Joanlennon: Well, I do a lot of school events and the kids mostly call me Joanlennon, one word.

JL: Joanlennon it is. Now, we're here to talk about your novel *Silver Skin*. I happen to know you dread the question, "What's your story about?" but I'm going to ask it anyway.

Joanlennon (deep breath): *Skara Brae, Orkney, the end of the Stone Age. The sun is dying, storms batter the coasts and people fear the end of the world. When Rab crawls out of the sea, wearing the remains of his Silver Skin, he throws the islanders into confusion. Who is he? Why has he come?*

JL: That sounds suspiciously like the blurb.

Joanlennon: I hoped you wouldn't notice. Okay, the three main characters are Rab, who lives in Orkney in a completely-urban far future and ends up in the Stone Age by accident; Voy, an angry old woman who lives in a time in decline and bitterly, passionately resents it; and Cait, who is in effect a refugee, rescued by Voy from the sea and bound to work for her.

JL: Set in Skara Brae, in Orkney, which is...?

Joanlennon: Which is...*amazing!* Orkney is a collection of islands just north of mainland Scotland, and on the west coast of the main island (called Mainland) is the Stone Age village of Skara Brae. I've been excited about it since I first saw *National Geographic* photos at the dentist, where I spent *way* too much time as a kid growing up in Canada. A village from before Stonehenge—from before the great pyramids at Giza—until one day, it disappeared, buried by sand, lost to all knowledge for thousands of years until, in 1850, a ferocious storm hit the islands like a hammer. The wind ripped the sand away and in the morning they discovered holes in the ground. And in the holes were small, perfect houses. They found a broken string of beads lying along the main passageway and mysterious carved stones you could hold in your hand and markings that looked like writing—hints everywhere...but where were the people? There weren't dead bodies strewn about the place like Pompeii, and yet so many of their belongings were still in place. What had *happened* here?

JL: So then and there, as a little girl with dubious dentition, you decided to write a book about it.

Joanlennon: Er, no. No, I grew up and did stuff and moved to Scotland. I visited Skara Brae a couple of times as a tourist and was completely bowled over—it is an astonishingly evocative site....

JL: *Then* you decided to write a book about it.

Joanlennon: Not...quite. No, the push to write a book about Skara Brae came when I was busily talking about something else entirely. I was in Orkney—in February, which shows grit, I feel—doing a series of events on *The Wickit Chronicles*, my books set in the Fens in medieval England, of all times/places. During a question and answer session, one of the pupils asked me why didn't I write a book set in Orkney? And *then* I realised I was desperate to do just that. The story of Rab and Cait and angry old Voy grew out of that moment.

JL: Finally! Talk about a slow boil. But you didn't mention the 1850s character.

Joanlennon: Rab from the far future and Cait and Voy from the Stone Age were there from the start, but the young Victorian bride Mrs. Trevelyan came into my head, quite quietly, later on in the writing. There's a rambling, bleak, cold, old house near Skara Brae that's open to the public—Skaill House—that I visited after I'd started work on the book. It had...an atmosphere. Mrs Trevelyan came out of that visit and became the voice of the framing chapters.

JL: And what *kind* of book is *Silver Skin*?

Joanlennon: Would you accept a "young adult/adult crossover science fiction historical adventure romance"? Somebody described it as "genre-bending" which I think sounds fabulous. Almost as if I'd planned it that way.

JL: *Did* you plan it that way?

Joanlennon: No. Sorry. It's just how the story came.

JL: Okay, here's a good one. Just exactly how historically accurate is *Silver Skin?*

Joanlennon: That *is* a good one, and so I wrote a Note to Readers on the last page of *Silver Skin.* It reads: So much of what we think we know about the time when the Stone Age was bleeding into the Bronze Age is based on bewildering artefacts and guesswork. What we do know, however, is that during this time, the climate worsened. There are many scientific, anthropological, archaeological theories about the effect climate change might have had on the civilization of the Orkney Islands, and I have cherry-picked indiscriminately among them. This story is just that—a story. It is driven by the interactions of fictional characters in a setting that has sparked my own imagination for years. I have researched and visited museums and sites and taken photographs and talked and listened, but if you are looking in the result for a historical document, you will be disappointed.

JL: Well, that works for me.

Joanlennon: You really are a very perspicacious interviewer.

JL: Cheers. Now, research…love it or loathe it?

Joanlennon: Love it…and fear it. I love throwing myself into a new time period and being wide open to anything and everything from scholarly pieces to popular interpretations to the out-there stuff. I particularly love those random discoveries you make that slot perfectly into the story, like the weird acoustics of the Ring of Brodgar or how bog cotton is good for packing wounds.

JL: And fear it?

Joanlennon: The thing I fear is that, after the book is done and splashing happily about out in the world, I'll read an article or watch a program that blows it out of the water! Of course I'm still fascinated by Skara Brae and Orkney. Of course I still want to go on learning. But I don't want to learn that something I put in *Silver Skin* has now been proven once and for all to be utterly totally completely *wrong*. *That's* scary.

JL: Last question: will there be a sequel to *Silver Skin*?

Joanlennon: No. It's a stand-alone book.

JL: Well, that's us done, I think. Fancy a coffee?

Joanlennon: Black, cold milk on the side?

JL: You read my mind.

~

JOAN LENNON is a Scottish-Canadian/Canadian-Scottish writer who lives in the top two floors of a Victorian house looking out over the River Tay. She has had novels, stories and poems published for readers of all ages. Her latest young adult novel, *Silver Skin*, is a sci-fi historical adventure romance set in Skara Brae, Orkney, mostly in the time when the Stone Age was bleeding messily into the Bronze Age. Joan is a member of The History Girls blog; more information on her and the book can be found at www.joanlennon.co.uk.

MICHELLE LOVRIC

~

The Venetian Novels

No matter what I *think* I'm going to write about, Venice always snatches the lead role in my novels. The following article shows just how she's got away with it. It's also about the characters from the past that I've inhabited while living and researching my books. I constantly walk around Venice "in costume," making my journeys inside the heads of my protagonists. They've each laid claim to different parts of the city and different points in history. Their memories have muddled with my own to the extent that sometimes I know who I am by *where* I am.

1. Perhaps no one will be surprised that I chose the lunatic asylum on the island of San Servolo as one of my favorite places in Venice— or that I've spent a lot of time there. Marcella Fasan, heroine of *The Book of Human Skin*, is falsely confined on San Servolo by her villainous brother Minguillo. Luigi Armiato, who curates the island's archives, allowed me to examine the sad ephemera of madness: the admission books, the *cartelle cliniche*, the photographs before and after treatment.

The mad no longer live on San Servolo. But on a wistfully misty day, using an old plan and our imaginations, Luigi Armiato and I paced out the former wings for the Furious and Tranquil Lunatics, the workshops, the bakery, the refectories. Part of the remaining structure is now a museum, which includes the old operating theater and the pharmacy, with its majolica jar of *theriaca*, Venetian Treacle. This drug, made of 70 ingredients including vipers, saves Renzo from Bubonic Plague in my children's novel *The Undrowned Child*.

2. For many years I rented an apartment in San Vio, and it is still my village. Yet in the last decade, it is has become much depleted. We used to have a *fruttivendolo*, a baker, two butchers, a haberdashery, a hardware store, a *latteria*: all lost. However, the heart of San Vio kept beating at Gino's, the bar where our hosts were the irreplaceable Emilio and Graziella Scarpa. They have now moved into a well-deserved retirement, but the place, still run by Venetians, has undergone a mild refurbishment and continues as ever. I've revised all my manuscripts at Gino's tables. And Cecilia Cornaro, portrait-painting heroine of *Carnevale*, has her studio 20 yards away. I use the present tense because Cecilia has appeared in three of my novels so far, and shows no sign of wishing to be left out of the next one.

3. The House of the Spirits is the setting for much of the mermaid action in *The Undrowned Child, The Mourning Emporium* and *The Fate in the Box*, three of my children's books. Originally a pleasure pavilion, the House of the Spirits is now home to retired nuns of the Cottolengo order. They kindly allowed me the run of the house and garden, and brought me a plastic chair to sit among the topiary

so I could write the scenes truly *in situ*. The nuns told me that the house's name derives from an uncanny echo that stirs the cypresses on windy nights. In the novel, the mermaids who protect Venice live in a cavern lined with golden mosaics hidden under the House of the Spirits. Of course they do. It seemed the only place in Venice romantic and secret enough for them.

4. I appropriated the garden of the Palazzo Zenobio for Valentine Greatrakes in *The Remedy*. And in a room beset by oversized stucco cupids, I found three chairs inquisitionally placed at the foot of my bed. They stand at the foot of Mimosina's bed in the same novel.

5. Sant'Alvise is where Pevenche ends up—Pevenche, the monstrous, misbegotten daughter of Tom in *The Remedy*. It's better that she deserves: Sant'Alvise is an enchanted place of high skies and silent streets. The convent's still inhabited by kindly nuns, who, if you are decently dressed, may permit you to roam the cloister and garden.

6. Fear of the famously haunted Ca' Dario almost destroys a marriage in *The Floating Book*. In *The Undrowned Child*, the smells of ink, varnish and blood ooze from its abandoned halls. A ghostly printing press stamps out the propaganda of a cruel new regime. And it's at Ca' Dario that my villain, Baiamonte Tiepolo, creates an army of Brustolon slave sculptures with leeches in their mouths.

7. Signor Rioba, perched on the edge of the Campo dei Mori, has long been one of my favorite "people" in Venice. One day, standing in the shade of that formidable iron nose, I heard an antiquated expletive inside my head. So I made Signor Rioba a warrior in *The Undrowned Child*, on the side of good, but rude enough to curse the bladder out of a weasel.

8. The back of the church of Santa Maria dei Miracoli is much more beautiful than the front, which seems to me like the fat-and-flesh cross-section you find exactly halfway through a *porchetta*. The side view of the bleached ribs of the church is my favorite in Venice. So I gave it to *Carnevale's* Cecilia Cornaro, whose bedroom faces it. As an artist, she would rejoice in it.

9. There's almost nothing that makes me happier than seeing an egret in Venice. They may be the angels that herald environmental apocalypse, but their ethereal grace actually makes Venice more beautiful. I've managed to ease an egret or two into *The Mourning Emporium*. In *Talina in the Tower*, my fiery eponymous heroine wages a characteristically colorful campaign against the slaughter of egrets for their feathers.

10. Possibly the one thing that makes me happier than egrets: gondola trips in famiglia—rowed by a close friend, Bruno Palmarin. His family have been gondoliers since 1742. If a gondolier makes a *giro* with friends or family, he forsakes his striped shirt and the boat's brass bling. When gondoliers glide past one another "at work," they exchange formal nods and greetings. But if they see a gondolier in famiglia, they burst into voluminous, affectionate Venetian patter, chatter and even song.

Is there a novelist immune to the lure of a gondola? Not this one. In *Carnevale*, Cecilia Cornaro is seduced in one. In *The Undrowned Child*, the gondoliers' children borrow their fathers' boats to ferry good ghosts out into the lagoon for the final battle against Baiamonte Tiepolo. In *The Floating Book*, Windelin and Lussieta Speyer row out into the lagoon to launch the first printed edition of Catullus symbolically, by casting a copy into the water.

11. I am very fascinated by Quintavalle, a remote part of Venice beyond San Pietro in Castello. I was taken there by local historian Lucio Sponza one warm summer evening, a time when the locals, cats and mosquitoes are at their most friendly. It's more real than any part of Venice, and yet not quite Venice either. I can't work it out. It niggles and teases. So I used it as the major setting for *Talina in the Tower*.

12. My twelfth location is the hidden back courtyard of the Conservatorio di Musica behind the Palazzetto Pisani. This is where I have often taken visitors at night, when their imaginations are already fevered by too much Venice and a little wine. I love the *frisson* of transgression in pushing open what seems to be a very private door. Through tall gates looms an architectural vista that's a mixture of Escher, Piranesi and Hogwarts. Staircases and loggias intertwine. Pasty statues leer in the moonlight. Sometimes an insomniac musician bleats a few plaintive notes on the flute. The morning after, I can easily convince my guests that they were dreaming it.

13. I've made this a baker's dozen. My last novel for adults, *The True & Splendid History of the Harristown Sisters*, was partly set in the sumptuous Palazzo Papadopoli. I was lucky enough to see it just before it was closed down and shrouded for a massive restoration. So I could choose the bedrooms of my sisters and even crouch on the floor to scribble my scenes, usually in one of the enfilades. The palazzo reopened a couple of years ago as the Aman Hotel, and George Clooney did me the honor of having his wedding party there. My guess is that he would have stayed in the bedroom of my heroine, Manticory, simply because no one could resist the mysterious *chinoiserie* of its frescoed walls. That's my theory, anyway.

MICHELLE LOVRIC's novels are always set at least partially in Venice. Her third novel, *The Remedy*, a mystery set against the background of 18th-century quack medicine, was long-listed for the Orange Prize. Her latest adult novels, *The Book of Human Skin* and *The True & Splendid History of the Harristown Sisters*, were published by Bloomsbury. Her novels for children, *The Undrowned Child* and *The Mourning Emporium* (Orion), feature the vengeful ghost of Venetian nobleman Baiamonte Tiepolo as their villain. They were followed by *Talina in the Tower* and *The Fate in the Box*. Find out more at www.michellelovric.com.

SARAH MCCOY

~

The Mapmaker's Children

*M*y husband can testify I am a horrible road-trip wing woman. Put a contemporary map in my hand, and I'll turn it topsy-turvy before I can decipher anything of travel assistance. The road names, byways, mile markers, and intersections all blend into a flurry of "Huh?" God forbid he ask me where the nearest gas station or fast-food joint might be. My traditional response: "Get off the interstate and we'll look around." We had a tent-revival *hallelujah* when we got our first GPS system.

But this isn't to say I don't like maps. Quite the contrary. I'm *obsessed* with them. They tickle my brain to think hard—harder.

I love that you can take a road map, strip it of boundaries, concrete highways, interstates, and exit numbers. Show me the topography of the land, the rivers and streams, mountain ranges and valleys, and suddenly, the world rises up off the page in vivid sensations: rocky, wet, and smelling of basin swamps and mountain air. It unspools —north, south, east, west. Each compass needle pointing to a story.

I'm particularly drawn to old maps. Visual atlases of how things were and are no more. The major road once connecting A to B is now gone. The major river once separating communities dried up fifty years back. Hilltops are laid low by our human wear and tear. Chunks of the earth are apportioned into territories/countries/ states then divided further. Wars shred the landscape, bearing something new—not worse or better, necessarily. Just changed.

And all the secret understanding is tucked into the mapmaker's key (also called the mapmaker's legend) at the bottom of the page, outside the plotted world; so if the journeyman is confused by the exact distance, surface, or body of water out of sight, the key will provide meaning.

Mapmaking: it's a skill *and* an art.

Despite my dunderhead beginnings, I became deeply reverent of maps through the writing of my latest novel, *The Mapmaker's Children*. We authors are story cartographers. We navigate characters, plot courses of action, and direct readers in an expedition across unfamiliar terrains. We *map* our fictional worlds using the storyteller's legend. Some writers might do this more formulaically with sticky notes, graphs, lists, and outlines, while others see it all from a bird's-eye view in their imagination. Sort of like the story mats and figurines I played with as a child: little painted pathways and mini-obstacles along the way to save the world.

While the creative process of plotting might be similar, it transforms dramatically based on the contextual elements of each story. The way I wrote *The Mapmaker's Children* was far different from the way I wrote my last.

For *The Mapmaker's Children*, I first outlined as "Sarah the author," an external omnipresence looking down into the historical diagram. Once intimately familiar with the two protagonists, I began to draw out the story as the characters would've seen and experienced it, free of presets and full of colors, shapes, and inventive forms. I interposed the structured lines (facts) with rich illusion (fiction).

I made miscalculations along the way—had to erase whole narrative trajectories and reroute. I learned that it's easy to become consumed by a corner, lost in the historical particulars of busy scenes, and fretful over getting the course of a river just right. But then, rivers and cities change. They are fluid and transmuting, just like humanity, life, and history. And so I pulled back to view the whole: the narrative in its moment of time for these unique characters.

It was an intense, magical process that I enjoyed, similar to the spellbound experience I have when running my finger along the ink grooves on old charts. It's the thrill of being a visual adventurer, being able to move across hundreds of thousands of miles with a gaze. It's the same thrill we get as readers engrossed in a time and place removed from our own.

When I was very young, I used the floor of my bedroom as a giant storyboard. I'd make up elaborate plots for my toy figurines: Barbie finds an imprisoned My Little Pony trapped in GI Joe's tower, and she must Speak & Spell correctly to free her plastic pink pal or lose her to the underworld of Garbage Pail Kids *foreverrrr*! I'm sure all of you, writer and reader friends, had similar dramatic playrooms.... or at least, I'll presume so here.

Before catching the school bus each morning, I'd set all my characters in their designated positions so the course of actions could take place. Then I'd dream all day about the dastardly challenges they faced, the triumphant celebrations, the new friends they'd pulled from my toy chest to join their exploits, and so forth. (It was my favorite game to play during math class.)

I'd rush home after school, disregarding my mom's warm cookies, a classmate's playground invitations, sing-along cartoons—straight to my secret world. I wanted to see what my characters had been up to in the hours I was missing, always convinced there would be evidence of their adventure somewhere....if I looked at the map carefully and closely enough. I was never disappointed.

I may still be an unreliable navigator on road trips with my husband, but not because I'm stumped. I'm just curious what lies off the demarcated streets, if only we were willing to get lost in the unknown. My husband would argue that this would defeat a map's purpose, but I like to think of it as merely the legend of possibilities.

~

SARAH MCCOY is the *New York Times, USA Today*, and international bestselling author of *The Mapmaker's Children; The Baker's Daughter*, a 2012 Goodreads Choice Award Best Historical Fiction nominee; the novella "The Branch of Hazel," featured in the anthology *Grand Central*; and *The Time It Snowed in Puerto Rico*. Sarah's work has been featured in *Real Simple, The Millions*, the *Huffington Post*, and other publications. She has taught English writing at Old Dominion University and at the University of Texas at El Paso. She calls Virginia home but presently lives in El Paso, Texas. Find out more about Sarah at www.sarahmccoy.com.

JAMES MCGEE

~

The Blooding

*I*t seemed like a good idea at the time: deciding, after penning three contemporary thrillers, to change genre. Cue drum roll. Four books later, staring at a blank screen, I couldn't help wondering what on earth had possessed me.

For me, writing's one of two things: a labor of love when it's going well or a pain in the proverbial when it's not. The process from conception to finished work has been compared to childbirth, save for a novelist there's usually a lot more kicking and screaming involved. A joke, ladies; please don't write in.

Looking back, *The Blooding* was a bit like that.

When I wrote *Hawkwood* I'd intended it to be a stand-alone novel. I hadn't envisaged a series. I wasn't sure I was up to the challenge, the main one being how to avoid the trap of regurgitating the same plot over and over again. Come on, you all know what I'm talking about; and no, I'm not going to name names.

When planning Matthew Hawkwood's fifth adventure, I knew I had to raise my game. At the end of the previous book, *Rebellion*, our hero was all at sea—literally. Having successfully evaded the clutches of the French police and blagged his way onto an American merchantman, the plan was for the vessel to be intercepted by the Royal Navy's blockade squadron, thus enabling him to hitch a ride back home.

Until I thought: Wouldn't it be a tad boring if I simply returned him to England? After all, he *was* on an American ship and America *was* at war with Britain. There had to be a story there somewhere.

The problem was that I knew very little about the War of 1812. Plus, there was another pressing matter to address: Hawkwood's background. Unfortunately, I knew even less about that than I did about the war. But then it occurred to me that if I could combine those two elements—the war and Hawkwood's origins—I might be able to kill two birds with one stone, so to speak.

Inspiration struck when I found myself re-watching Michael Mann's adaptation of James Fenimore Cooper's *The Last of The Mohicans* and I thought: *Whoa!* This could be a great opportunity to take Hawkwood's story to a new level, as there's nothing in any of the previous books to suggest the history I had now decided to give him.

But where to start?

Ask the average Brit when their country was at war with America— not counting that revolutionary spat—and the likelihood is you'll be met with a blank stare. The same might even apply to some Americans and Canadians, even though the War of 1812 played a huge part in their history.

Fortunately, there's no shortage of reference material, both in print and in cyberspace. Donald Hickey's *The War of 1812: A Forgotten Conflict* and Carl Benn's *The Iroquois in the War of 1812* were my go-to reference books. They were an invaluable source of material and the basis for all my subsequent web searches.

But, my goodness, there's an awful lot of chaff out there and you can spend hours poring over stuff you'll never use, not to mention there's the serious risk you'll bore your readers rigid with too much— for that, read tedious—historical detail.

The Hawkwood novels are based on real events, so how was I going to familiarize readers with the period background while at the same time and, more importantly, hold their attention? When it comes to historical fiction, the story has to resonate with today's readership. Otherwise, what's the point? A decent plot, therefore, is only half the battle. If you've got no stimulating characters, your story is, frankly, dead in the water.

Excluding real people such as—among others—Sir John Johnson and Zebulon Pike, the Kanien'kehá:ka (Mohawk) were always the driving force in the narrative. Hawkwood's personality is forged by his boyhood relationship with the Mohawk war captains Tewanias and Cageaga, and so their portrayal was critical. I borrowed their names from Kanien'kehá:ka warriors of the time, and I freely admit that Tewanias was based partly on Fenimore Cooper's wonderful creation Chingachgook.

As for the landscape, the Adirondacks are a spectacular setting and were crucial to the plot due to the influence they had on the historic events upon which the novel is based.

That was where my research took off. I was able to make use of war and travel journals from the period along with some terrific websites dedicated to Iroquois history and culture. I also received tremendous help from museums and historical societies. Between thee and me, I think they were impressed that a Limey was requesting information on American and Canadian history!

Which brings us to the question: Are there advantages to writing historical as opposed to contemporary fiction? The somewhat trite answer is that with historical fiction you're rarely overtaken by events. New research, sure, but, generally speaking, it's usually down to a fresh interpretation of already known facts.

Writers who pen modern adventure tales all have a cricked neck from looking over their shoulders for fear of the headlines coming up behind them. You do wonder how many have just typed *The End* only to turn on the evening news to find that a breaking story has just turned 300 pages of carefully crafted prose into cat litter. Heartbreaking doesn't come anywhere near it.

For *The Blooding*, it took two years to write and nine months to transform the manuscript into the finished word. Scroll back through the news bulletins during that near-three-year period and note how the world changed (and not for the better, many would say).

So, do I write historical fiction because it's easier? No, because it ain't. It's because I love history. I didn't when I was at school; I found it a chore. I like to think that was due to less-than-charismatic teachers rather than my inadequacies, but I could be wrong. It was through reading historical fiction that my imagination was fired, encouraging me to investigate the real events lurking behind all those wonderful tales.

And maybe that's why we historical fiction writers do take pen to paper. Well, it sure ain't for the dosh! I like to think it's in the hope that if just one reader has been grabbed by our lowly efforts and been encouraged to explore the past for themselves, it will have been worth it. And what if he or she then took up his or her own pen and wondered: What if...?

Now, there's a thought....

~

Born into an army family, **JAMES MCGEE** grew up in Gibraltar, Germany and Northern Ireland. He has worked in banking, newspaper sales and the airline industry—for both British Airways and Pan Am—and as a store manager for two of Britain's leading booksellers. The five novels in the Hawkwood series are *Hawkwood, Resurrectionist, Rapscallion, Rebellion* and *The Blooding*. His other novels are *Trigger Men, Crow's War* and *Wolf's Lair*. When not involved in philosophical discourse with his laptop, he loves movies, travel and Bruce Springsteen, but not necessarily in that order. He lives in Somerset, England. Find out more at www.jamesmcgee.uk.

CINDY RINAMAN MARSCH

Rosette

*J*opened the antique journal, a small, mottled brown version of our modern composition books, and saw feathery faded-to-brown ink on every page. The script "Rosette Cordelia Ramsdell Journal No. 14 1856" headed the first diary entry, and the next line read "Lyons, Ionia Co. Mich." Rosette Ramsdell attended a teachers institute at age 26 that September, and the following pages of the journal tell of her daily life over the next 18 months as she prepares to marry, moves into a shanty home, and gives birth to her first child. Rosette's family prospered with the production of maple sugar, her father led the local Republican delegation to vote for Fremont, and her brother Solomon played his fiddle at local dances. Rosette records, too, the popular novels she read—one about Revolutionary War pirates.

On the 45th page, in the formal flowery language of the time, Rosette records her marriage to Otis Churchill. But near the bottom of the page, where she celebrates his character and the day, the precise brown ink has been altered with a pencil, so that it contradicts that praise.

This shocking edit was the origin of my novel *Rosette: A Novel of Pioneer Michigan*. My mother, who died in 2013, found the journal in a thrift shop and gave it to me, pointing out page 45 and saying, "You need to write this story." As I squinted at the delicate hand-writing, I was drawn into Rosette's world of sewing, harvests, and a honeymoon by sleigh. I searched for clues to the change that would come later, but the journal does not reveal anything explicitly. Rosette records events and the occasional poetic description of snow or smoke. She rarely tells of her own feelings, though her vivid dreams of teaching classrooms of girls with beards or of following shady characters into deep caverns would have kept Freud busy.

I had nothing more of Rosette's journals—not the first 13 volumes nor any that followed the 14th. But as I began researching her life and the lives of family members and neighbors named in the journal, her story solidified. Each birth, death, plat map, and legal record told me a little more about this woman who died in 1913 at age 83. As I completed the first full draft of the novel, a genealogist friend found a court document that confirmed more fully what I had supposed. And as the novel approached its publication date, I came across two letters to the editor of the women's department of a magazine— Rosette had written them in her sixties. Those letters revealed yet more of her character, and I was pleased that I'd gotten things right.

This novel suggested itself from an unknown life—I have no letters, no photos nor reminiscences of her children or grandchildren. But the journal itself is rich with suggestion, and it was a delight to delve and ponder, to consider what might have been left out. In fact, one of those magazine letters gives a detail of Rosette's wedding day that she does not record in the journal. The novel itself became a living document fed by history as well as by my own imagination—it came to life beneath my typing fingers.

The historical timeline gave me a framework within which to work. I knew I needed a "grabbing" first chapter, and Rosette's sedate attendance at a teachers' meeting wasn't going to do the job. So the novel begins years later with a scene that explains the editing of that journal page. The reader's task then, knowing Rosette has changed the journal, is to follow along the details of her life to discover just where the seeds of disaster might have been sown. We squirm as we read of the Rosette living in the earlier years of the novel—she does not know what is coming.

The final product is a novel faithful to the details in the journal and to what I have of the history. But just as two family members might differently recall a relationship or an event, and perhaps embellish the memory consciously or unconsciously, so I have encountered these lives and come away with my own thoughts. *Rosette* does not provide definitive interpretations but, like life, offers ambiguity and tendency. Therein lies my own fascination with Rosette. I am content when readers finish the book with the same sense I have of being just a little off-balance. Rosette will not soon leave our minds and hearts.

⁓

CINDY RINAMAN MARSCH has taught writing in colleges and online to secondary students for over 30 years before beginning her own writing career. She and her physics professor husband

Glenn have raised and educated their four grown children and enjoy their garden and hobby winery in Western Pennsylvania. *Rosette: A Novel of Pioneer Michigan* (January 2016) is her first published work. Find out more at www.rosettebook.com.

MIRANDA MILLER

Loving Mephistopheles

*M*y fifth novel is a literary fantasy, a 21st-century retelling of the story of Faust in a story that spans several previous centuries. All my novels are triggered by images, and this one began with the mental picture of a young woman with a pale, rather Gothic face and long black curly hair, reflected in a brandy balloon she was staring into at an airport. Somehow I knew that she was not really young and that her name was Jenny.

I was in my mid-forties and had just been through treatment for breast cancer. I didn't want to write about this directly, but my encounter with my own mortality changed me. Over the next four years my first marriage broke up and my mother, brother and father all died. I think that writing about a woman who didn't die was a gesture of defiance I desperately needed. I'd always been told my novels don't fit into any particular genre, and for some time I'd felt frustrated by the restrictions of the realistic novel. The time was ripe to act on that.

In 1996, I saw the wonderful Royal Shakespeare Company production of Howard Brenton's adaptation of Goethe's *Faust*, with
Michael Feast as Faust and Hugh Quarshie as Mephistopheles. I
read all the versions of this legend I could lay my hands on: *Don
Juan, Don Giovanni*, Marlowe's *Doctor Faustus* and more. I wanted
to modernize and feminize the legend and I became fascinated by
the idea that women are no longer allowed to grow old. In legend,
eternal youth is a magical quest, but it was beginning to be possible
to replace almost every part of your body scientifically. So I wanted
my Jenny to span a long period, from the 19th century to the future.

My other novels have taken an average of three years to write and
I usually write at least three drafts. This one, however, was written
over about nine years and I can no longer remember how many
different versions I wrote. At one point it was going to be a trilogy,
but it ended up as one long and rather sprawling volume. After I
moved from Oxford to London, in 2002, I abandoned *Loving Mephistopheles* for about three years and wrote an (unpublished) autobiographical novel called *Family Portrait*. But Jenny and Leo had
tremendous vitality, they wouldn't leave me alone. Different versions
of *Loving Mephistopheles* were rejected by many publishers and my
agent, understandably, lost patience with me.

I became more and more interested in Leo, my Mephistopheles,
and decided to write some of the novel from his point of view. I
wanted him to have an identity crisis as belief in Christianity faded
and he began to be mortal, with real feelings and a decaying body.
The love story between Jenny and Leo was intended to reflect some
of the ways that relations between the sexes changed over the course
of the 20th century.

In the back of my mind when I was writing this novel was my paternal grandmother, Florence Esme Hyman, who died before I was born. We grew up with stories about her dramatic rise from poverty in a Jewish immigrant family in Wales. She was shipped out to South Africa with the fishing fleet, married a shopkeeper in Kimberley and had two little girls, who she abandoned to return to England with a rich stockbroker. My father was born in the middle of her divorce and grew up in England, in lavish surroundings. The money was all spent long ago, but the stories lived on, and I felt I knew this beautiful, rapacious, witty woman. When I was eight and had a fever, I hallucinated her, dressed in black, lurking in our toilet with a gun, waiting to kill my mother.

I can break down the different sections of the novel to see where they came from: Jenny's music hall career came out of my failed childhood ambition to act and my lifelong fascination with the theatre; the Second World War scenes were based on my parents' stories of London during the Blitz; my Metaphysical Bank grew out of the Banca del Santo Spirito, a title which amused me when I lived in Rome, and out of my own humiliation at being in debt for most of the 1990s—it was easy to villainize a bank. I'm a passionate Italophile and Italy has snuck into most of my novels, so that's why Jenny goes to live in Rapallo, and the druggy chapters, when Leo becomes a cocaine dealer, have their roots in my own misspent youth in London in the 1960s. Jenny and Abbie's experience of homelessness continues my train of thought when I was writing my first and last non-fiction book, *Bed and Breakfast: Women and Homelessness Now* (Women's Press 1990). As for the future, that's anybody's guess, and the guessing is fun.

That's a rational analysis of a novel that didn't feel at all rational while I was writing it. I wouldn't describe it as a historical novel, though it visits many moments in time, but as a fantastic story I told myself to help me through a difficult period, a kind of maze I had to fight my way out of.

I haven't reread *Loving Mephistopheles* since it was published (I can't bear to reread my own books) and its publication still seems somewhat miraculous. Peter Owen had published my stories about Saudi Arabia, *A Thousand and One Coffee Mornings*. I knew that he liked my work and that his editor, his daughter Antonia, shared my love of fantasy. So I decided to make one last attempt and sent it off to them. If anybody reading this has, like me, been told by agents and publishers that your novel is unfashionable and unpublishable, don't give up! Peter Owen published the novel in 2006, and I am grateful for it still.

~

MIRANDA MILLER has published seven novels, most recently *Loving Mephistopheles* (2006), *Nina in Utopia* (2010) and *The Fairy Visions of Richard Dadd* (2013). *King of the Vast*, the final volume of her Bedlam Trilogy, will be published in 2016. She has also published a volume of short stories and a book of interviews with homeless women and politicians. Her next novel will be set in the art world in 18th-century Rome and London. She blogs for The History Girls and works for The Literary Consultancy as a reader and mentor. She has a daughter and two stepchildren and lives in London with her second husband. Her website is www.mirandamiller.info.

JUDITH CLAIRE MITCHELL

A Reunion of Ghosts

J first heard of Fritz Haber in 1998, when I caught a snippet of a TV documentary about 20th-century scientists. The camera zoomed in on an image of a bald man in a military uniform, a pair of *pince nez* clamped to the bridge of his nose. He looked like a stereotypical German nationalist circa World War I, and that's exactly what he turned out to be: a militaristic Prussian, this chemist whose devotion to the fatherland was so unwavering he had no qualms about creating and deploying the first chemical weapons used in battle. What difference did it make whether someone died from a bullet or from the long, cruel death that ensues after inhaling gas?

"Dead is dead," said Fritz Haber.

The documentary also mentioned Fritz's wife, Clara. A chemist, too, she was kept out of the lab and relegated instead to a life of *Küche* and *Kinder*. She spent her last years railing against her husband's deadly work until, unable to sway him, she killed herself. The morning she died, Fritz Haber obeyed the Kaiser's orders and traveled to the Eastern Front. The Habers' 12-year-old son was left to bury his mother.

A compelling personal story and a story about the 20th century. Chemical warfare, sexism, world war, imperialism, and, because the Habers were born Jewish, the specter of Nazism, exile, diaspora.

"Wow," I said to my husband. "A book about those two would write itself."

The documentary went on to another scientist, and I went on with whatever I was doing that day, most likely working on my first novel, which was definitely not writing itself. But even as I threw myself into my work, I knew I was already obsessed with these Habers. I knew my next book would be about them.

I even knew what that next book would look like. None of this business of coming up with an original plot. My next novel would be a *roman à clef*. By definition, its plot would simply be a retelling of the verifiable details of Fritz and Clara's lives. Oh, I'd flesh things out by giving them deeply imagined inner lives, and I'd try to make the sentences lovely and lyrical. But basically, I'd just be doing one of those ripped-from-the-headlines kind of narratives.

Without the need to concoct an intricate plot, I told some writer friends over cocktails, the book would take no time at all.

"A book like that would practically write itself," said one of these friends, the most famous in the group, who was either being sincere or sarcastic. It was hard to tell with her.

I decided to go with sincere. I was worry-free when I back-burnered Fritz and Clara. I knew I'd come back to them eventually, and when I did it would take no more than a year, maybe just a few months, for the book to write itself.

The truth is, though, that while I turned the flame down low, I never turned it off completely. Every now and then I'd take a brief break from writing or teaching—I was teaching now, too—and sneak in a little research on my chemists.

That's when I discovered a problem. It turned out there was very little information about Fritz Haber out there and almost none about Clara. Also, what little there was seemed to be mostly in German. How was I to figure out the day-to-day of their lives without biographies and articles and letters in English?

"You can't," the most famous writer said. This time there was no question she meant it.

I was annoyed and embarrassed. I'd forgotten to specify that when my book wrote itself, it needed to do so in English.

A few years passed. The first novel was published. The teaching was going well. I was gaining confidence, was less dependent on the opinions of others. When I turned back to the Habers, I did so with renewed energy. My obsession still burned. All I had to figure out now was how to proceed.

An idea occurred. I would write whatever the opposite of a *roman à clef* is. Instead of writing about Fritz and Clara Habers' real lives, I'd write about their wholly invented afterlives. Fritz and Clara, dead and waiting to see if they were going to be allowed into heaven: that would be the book. It would be super-fictionalized, fantastical. I'd even throw in a bunch of other historical figures. Whose sins would be forgiven? Who would be forever damned?

Not only did this book not write itself, but it put its foot down and wouldn't let me write it either. I tried, but everything I put on the page was clunky and fake. I just didn't have the imagination for this kind of thing.

The good news was that while I'd been biding my time and spinning my wheels, the research landscape had been changing. The most important of the German biographies had been translated into English. A new biography—also in English—had been published. Feminists and scholars were writing about Clara. The cyber highway, barely existent when I'd first heard of the Habers, was now bumper to bumper with articles about both of them.

I should have been happy. With all this material, I could return to my *roman à clef*. The book that would write itself could finally get down to work.

And yet here was the thing: I no longer wanted to spend time on a book that could write itself. I'd lost interest in telling a story I now knew inside and out. Why would I want to write a book when I knew how it ended?

After all this time something that should have been obvious from the start finally coalesced. I didn't want to write about Fritz and Clara Haber. I wanted to write about me.

That is, I wanted to know why I, a person living in such a different time and place, a person who stopped studying science after 10th-grade biology, was so obsessed with these two chemists. What was it about their lives and legacies that wouldn't leave me alone? Did their stories trigger fear? Grief? Something else that I couldn't yet name or wouldn't yet admit to?

I was implicated now in their story, and that's what it took. Not only did I no longer want the book to write itself, but I no longer wanted to write it from the perspective of Fritz or Clara or even that abandoned 12-year-old. I wanted my narrator to be someone like me. I needed to find someone—invent someone—who shared my obsession and also my questions.

I invented not one but three narrators, sisters born around the same time as me, who lived in the city where I once lived. Their maternal great-grandparents had been chemists who'd lived pretty much the same external lives as Fritz and Clara Haber. But they weren't Fritz and Clara Haber. They were Lenz and Iris Alter. When I gave them those names, made that Alter-ation as my pun-crazy narrators would say, the nature of my project became clear to me, and much of the plot fell in place.

Something interesting happened then. One day, doing some minor fact checking, I searched the names Fritz and Clara Haber and noticed among the familiar links one for a family tree I'd never before encountered. When I clicked on it, I saw that it included the Habers' great-grandchildren.

A moment before I'd known nothing of this generation, was busily making it up. Now I had names, dates, cities. A few more clicks and I had contact info for a great-granddaughter who lived in England and welcomed correspondence from anyone interested in Fritz Haber.

And so we exchanged emails. She was lovely and generous and happy to help me, though I'd already done so much research, there was little new she could tell me.

I didn't stop writing to her because she had no revelations to share. I stopped writing for the opposite reason. I was afraid she'd eventually tell me something she'd want me to include in my book. I feared she'd have a point of view that she'd want me to express. I was concerned I'd get to like her and become protective of her sensibilities. I was scared of pulling my punches, of being polite, of allowing my Alters to revert to Habers.

I'd once worried about a dearth of research material. Now I'd found a primary source and what did I do? I walked away. It was all right. The book was coming along. I knew that because I was, at last, writing it myself.

~

JUDITH CLAIRE MITCHELL is the author of the novels *The Last Day of the War* and *A Reunion of Ghosts*. She teaches undergrad and graduate fiction workshops at the University of Wisconsin, where she is a professor of English and the director of the M.F.A. program in creative writing. She has received grants and fellowships from the Michener-Copernicus Society of America, the Wisconsin Institute for Creative Writing, the Wisconsin Arts Board, and Bread Loaf, among others. Find out more at www.judithclairemitchell.com.

CHRIS NICKSON

~

Leeds, The Biography:
A History of Leeds in Short Stories

L eeds is my hometown, the place where I've returned to live after many years away. I've written about it at many different stages in its growth. My Richard Nottingham series takes place in the 1730s, just as the town is beginning to grow rich off the wool trade, although there are still fewer than 10,000 people there. The Tom Harper series of the 1890s sees an industrial behemoth that's spread wide, while by the 1950s of my Dan Markham, Leeds is a thoroughly modern metropolis.

I'd made two separate attempts to write a crime novel set in Leeds during the English Civil War. On one of them I passed 35,000 words before I finally had to admit that it simply wasn't coming alive properly. Time to give up.

But the raw material was certainly there. A battle in a snowstorm saw the Roundheads take control of the place as leading supporters of the King took flight. Some revenge, knocking down the houses of the supporters of King Charles until the main street, Briggate, looked gap-toothed. A garrison running the place, a city occupied. And then, several months later, in March 1645, the first case of plague, a young girl from a very poor area. Over the next nine months, until the disease finally passed, more than 1,300 people would die. The army would have to erect plague cabins to isolate the sick. It was quite a backdrop for the story of Roundhead versus Cavalier.

But I still couldn't make the book work.

What *did* work, a little later, was a short story called "Little Alice Musgrave", named for the plague's first victim and told 20 years later by her mother. When I finished, I realized it said many of the things I'd wanted to say in the novel, but this version was more powerful for being so concentrated and focused.

In recent years I've written novels, and those have taken my time. But with "Little Alice Musgrave" I saw how I could use the short story to write a very different history of Leeds from the ones that fill my bookshelves. There are limits to how many eras a single novel can cover. In short stories, I could look at them all. As far as I'm aware, no one's done this for a place, not in short stories—probably no one was foolish enough to attempt it. There was certainly enough to go at, dating back to the possibility of some small Roman occupation all the way to now.

Fragments of history, folktales, little comments: All those are grist to the mill for a writer. Particularly for a collection like this. The first story, set in 363 AD, came from a note I'd seen. A little after 1900, in one of the suburbs, men were excavating to build a large new house. They came on a stone sarcophagus, which was established as Roman. It hadn't been disturbed, but when they opened it there were only two bones inside. Why? Who would go to all the trouble and expense to bury *two bones*? I wanted to know—and so I made up my own answer.

There were plenty of other starting places. A young woman who supposedly walked down some stone stairs into the river in the 1800s, the place (which no longer exists) becoming known locally as Jenny White's Hole. Folktale or fact? It didn't really matter, but what might have made her do something like that?

After the North of England proved unwilling to submit to William the Conqueror, he sent troops to devastate the place. In the Domesday Book, manor after manor is listed as "waste." Leeds itself escaped; the places immediately around it weren't so lucky. What would the "Harrying of the North" be like for someone on the receiving end? History doesn't always need to be written by the victors.

In fact, that was part of the point. Over the centuries, who knows how many thousands, even millions, of people have lived in Leeds. Most of them died forgotten, without any memorial, at best a name in a parish register or on a gravestone. The stories offered a way to commemorate a few of them. Not just the great and the good, but the ordinary people who spent their lives below the radar of history. The crippled and the dying who take part in a food riot of my story "Lady Ludd." The shopgirl working in the brand new department store of "Wonderland." The member of the Town Waits, or musicians, who also happens to be part of the Night Watch and learns that Bonnie Prince Charlie and his army have crossed over from Scotland on Bonfire Night, 1745. Each story tells one of their tales, with an historical note for context.

By the time I was done, I had 30 stories in total. A small local publisher brought them out under the title *Leeds, The Biography: A History of Leeds in Short Stories.*

It is, perhaps, a biography of this place that fascinates me.

More to the point, there are plenty more Leeds tales to tell.

~

CHRIS NICKSON was born and raised in Leeds. He has a love affair with the city, exploring it in fiction over several different periods. A crime writer and music journalist, he spent 30 years in the US, many in Seattle, before returning to the UK, finally settling contentedly just a mile from where he grew up. In novels he writes the places and people he feels in his bones. With music he prefers the paths that aren't as well trodden, that lead to other parts of the globe. Find out more about Chris's work at www.chrisnickson.co.uk.

J.L. OAKLEY

The Jøssing Affair

*W*here do ideas for historical novels come from? Sometimes it's a letter found in a research box, a family tale, or a photograph. Sometimes, the idea could be triggered by a dream.

"He found the young man lying in the snow, his battered body pushed deep under the brambles at the bottom of a ravine. If it had not been for the sound of the car door slamming, Hans Gunnerson would never have found him." This is how my World War II novel, *The Jøssing Affair*, opens, just as I dreamed it nearly 25 years ago. After I told a friend about it, she told me to write it down. I did. She loved it and said to do more. I never had written a novel before. Worse, I knew nothing about Norway during World War II beyond Steinbeck's *The Moon is Down* and the 1965 Kirk Douglas film *The Heroes of Telemark*. But the man in the snow and some long-ago plot I had toyed with with kept coming back, eventually pushing me to write *The Jøssing Affair*.

The novel takes place in the last year of World War II, when British-trained Norwegian intelligence agent Tore Haugland is a jøssing—a patriot—sent to a fishing village on Norway's west coast to set up a line to receive weapons and agents from England via the clandestine operation known as the Shetland Bus. Posing as a deaf fisherman, his mission is complicated when he falls in love with Anna Fromme, a German widow with secrets of her own.

But it took a long time to get from my dream to a finished book. The process began in earnest when my historian instincts kicked in. I went to the library, because back then there was no Internet. In short order, I found out some basic facts about Norway in 1940. With three million people, it was the smallest country, popula-tion-wise, in Europe; in fact, the city of Berlin alone had a larger population. The fishing and maritime industries dominated the country's commerce, with especially rich fisheries in the north. The rural communities on the west coast were tied together by coastal ferry and often had their own dialects; during the novel's time period, each might have had only one phone and no electricity. Trondheim, Bergen and Oslo were Norway's leading centers of culture and ed-ucation; all three cities were attacked by Germans on a single day, April 9, 1940.

When researching a subject, it's always good to read an overview of the times and then explore the bibliography in the back of the book. Yes, books can still give you all sorts of leads into your research. The first book I discovered was a collection of stories about occupied Norway called *Blood on the Midnight Sun*. Written by the Danish-born American writer and World War II veteran Hans Christian Adamson, it was a gold mine, eventually leading me to four story strands for my novel: the Shetland Bus Operation; the razing of a little fishing village called Televåg; the activities of Norway's Minister for the Deaf, pastor Conrad Bonnevie-Svendsen; and the man who would be my villain, Henry Oliver Rinnan, Norway's number-two war criminal during World War II.

The story began to flow, but work on it proceeded more slowly than it might today. With no Internet, I ordered books for my research through inter-library loan. And with no computer, I wrote the manuscript by hand for the first two years.

An exceptional find was two volumes of the Naval Intelligence Division (NID) Geographic Handbook for Norway. These Handbooks were fully classified during the War, as they were designed by the British Admiralty to provide information for British armed forces—in this case, for agents going to Norway. (It was at the Geographical Division of the NID that author Ian Fleming worked for a while.) Found on a shelf at my local university library, the handbooks cover culture and history and include an amazing array of train schedules, maps, and photographs that helped me to create an authentic background for the intelligence agent in my story.

Another valuable find were members of the Norwegian Men's Choir in my area. The men and women I interviewed had all lived in occupied Norway in their twenties. Their experiences with rationing, daily life under the Germans and the local NS (the Norwegian Nazi Party), forced labor, and their memories of tragic incidents in their towns and villages, lent another layer of authenticity to my story.

One of my favorite discoveries was learning that during the War Norway had cars that ran on wood or charcoal, called *knottgenerator*.

In wartime, only Germans or member of the NS were permitted to use gasoline. One interviewee told me how he and his family would go to the local gas station and pick up bags of charcoal or wood to put into the furnace on the back on their vehicle. Using this ingenious method, a car could run at about 30-40 miles an hour, getting about 20 miles to a bag of fuel, though I confess that I forget the precise estimate.

I was also fascinated with the role that Conrad Bonnevie-Svendsen, the Norwegian Minister for the Deaf, played in the resistance effort. The pastor would travel around the country visiting the various churches and schools for the deaf, then hold secret meetings with members high in the resistance movement. This was a lucky break for my main character, intelligence agent Tore Haugland, since he is posing as a deaf fisherman. The novel reveals a backstory that ties him to Bonnevie-Svendsen and the Church of Norway's congregations for the deaf and hearing impaired. Of course, to write this aspect of the novel well, I had to try to understand what deaf culture was like in Norway. A letter from the head priest of the congregation for the deaf introduced me to someone who had known Conrad Bonnevie-Svendsen.

Finally, there is the so-called Shetland Bus, one of the most celebrated clandestine operations in Norway's World War II history. It started out as a collection of fishing boats going back and forth between Norway and the Shetland Islands under cover of winter darkness, transporting arms and agents. In 1943, the Norwegian government received three submarine chasers—the *Hitra*, *Vegra* and *Hessa*—and dedicated them to the operation. It was dangerous work, not only because of its risky transports but also due to the turbulent storms that were common in the North Sea; despite those dangers, it ran so regularly that it earned its affectionate nickname, the Shetland Bus. Working with a curator at Resistance Museum in Oslo, I was able to get timetables of the boats coming to western Norway to tie in with the timeline of my novel. Today, there is one boat left, the restored MV *Hitra*, and the Shetland Bus remains one of the great stories of World War II adventure and heroism.

Over time, I became active on the Internet with various groups who study World War II, particularly individuals who are knowledgeable about the occupation of Norway and the country's five grueling years under German and Nazi authority. I continue to learn and seek out the latest in articles, historical exhibits and popular culture about Norway. Just as important, people continue to share their family stories.

As I mentioned, *The Jøssing Affair* is my first novel. With it I learned how to write a novel, query it, pitch it, and send it out into the world. It won awards, got full reads and high interest, but there was always some reason for a publisher not to take it on. In many ways, I'm glad that it ended up being my third published novel because in the interim I learned how to care for it and get into the right hands.

When it launched at Village Books on April 9, 2016—the 76th anniversary of the German invasion of Norway—I noticed people crying in the audience. I'm not sure if that is a good thing (though someone told me that it was), but when I heard that, I knew that I had touched readers. It's very rewarding when someone writes to tell me that they recommended *The Jøssing Affair* to their book club because the novel is the most authentic thing they have read about World War II in Norway as they personally experienced it.

What better tribute could an author of historical fiction ask for?

~

Award-winning author J.L. OAKLEY writes historical fiction that spans the mid-19th century to World War II. Her novels include *The Tree Soldier*, set in the Pacific Northwest during the 1930s, and *Timber Rose*, as well as *The Jøssing Affair*. Recent recognition includes a 2015 Silver WILLA Literary Award for historical fiction. When not writing, she demonstrates 19th-century folkways to school-age children at national parks and museums. Find out more at www.historyweaver.wordpress.com.

CHARLES PALLISER

~

The Quincunx, The Unburied, and Rustication

I write fiction set in the 19th century as a way of understanding the present. (And from other motives, as I admit below.) The Victorian setting is a mirror that, when we look into it, both distorts our faces and yet tells us the truth.

The process of writing a novel is a means of finding out what I already think and feel about a range of topics but have not made explicit to myself. And in the process of writing, I hope to find that assumptions I've made more or less unreflectingly are mistaken, because that is a thrilling discovery. Nothing is more exciting than having to rethink matters one has assumed have been settled. And ideally I hope to let the reader share that process and perhaps similarly challenge what has been taken for granted.

When I started working on *The Quincunx* one of my main preoccupations was this cluster of related questions: What is one's relation to the circumstances in which one comes into consciousness as a child? How does one accept or reject the values of the family and the society in which one is raised? How does one work out one's course in life? Are our deepest beliefs instilled in us at so early an age that they cannot be altered? How can one distinguish the desire for justice from the hunger for revenge?

By setting those questions in the 19th century I made them both clearer and more complex than if I had used a setting from my own lifetime. In both that novel and my most recent one, *Rustication*, I put a specific family situation back into the 19th century, and that meant that I had to sort out the essential psychological issues from what are merely contextual factors. In the more recent book I examined what it was to be a somewhat troubled boy of 17 almost exactly one hundred years earlier than I was one myself. I found that it pretty well all fitted: the sense that one's family were malign strangers, the temptation to drink and drug, the pressures of sexual desire, the anger at the pettiness and spite of adult society, etc. (Not everything matched. Unlike a modern teenager, my character is additionally oppressed by the realization that his mother and sister depend on him for their financial wellbeing. Family responsibilities of that kind are, with some exceptions, no longer imposed on the young in modern societies.) In *Rustication* I found a situation that I felt was a metaphor for the classic teenage feeling that the adults around one know facts that have a bearing on oneself but they are deliberately keeping them secret. The "hero" of my novel finds out that some very dark truths are being concealed from him but that they are known by numerous malicious gossips in the claustrophobic society he is living in.

In both novels (as well as in my other "Victorian novel," *The Unburied*) the imitation of 19th-century fiction allowed me to make greater use of melodrama than would have seemed appropriate if I had been using a modern setting. And related to that, though it's a very different point, is the fact that the historical setting permitted me to put my characters through more extreme experiences than would have been plausible in a late-20th-century context. In *The Quincunx* I created an affectionate parody of Victorian fiction that featured a madhouse, a brothel, a gang of grave robbers, sewer scavengers, etc.

What did I learn in using that setting? I gradually realized that my "hero" in *The Quincunx* had to have suffered psychological and moral damage in ways I had not anticipated when I was in the early stages of working on the novel. The book became a study of the harm that one inflicts on oneself if one allows oneself to be trapped by the injustices of one's early life. In *Rustication* I explored the inevitable cost of trying to break out of those traps.

Of course, I can't pretend that I use a Victorian setting only because I want to investigate issues that press in on me in my own life. I also want to explore that period because I'm fascinated by it, and particularly by its mixture of familiarity and strangeness. People who are only three or four generations from us can at one moment sound exactly like us and at the next moment astonish us with an attitude—to gender, or race, or class, or colonialism—that seems incomprehensible. Above all, I want to think about the ways in which the image we have of the 19th century from the fiction of that period misrepresents the reality by a process of distortion and omission. That sounds arrogant. Am I putting Dickens and the Brontës on trial for failing to condemn the injustices of their age that seem so obvious to us? Almost the opposite. By seeing how different their vision of themselves is from our perspective on them, I can glimpse the ways in which our own age suffers blind spots and is seduced by its own propaganda. Can we condemn the Victorians for stepping around people dying on their streets when we flick our television's news channels from one horror to another, looking for entertainment? We find ways to deal with the contradictions and injustices around us just as effectively as our great-grandparents did. So again it comes back to the idea that the 19th century is a distorting mirror in which we see another image of ourselves, and one that we might not like.

CHARLES PALLISER was born in Massachusetts but has lived in the UK since the age of three. A graduate of Oxford University, he writes full time in London. His debut novel, *The Quincunx*, became an international bestseller and was awarded the Sue Kaufman Prize for First Fiction by the American Academy and Institute of Arts and Letters, given for the best first novel published in North America. His subsequent books include *The Sensationist, Betrayals, The Unburied,* and *Rustication*, which appeared in 2013 and was chosen as one of *Publishers Weekly's* Best Books of the Year.

ALYSSA PALOMBO

~

The Violinist of Venice

he first seed of inspiration for *The Violinist of Venice* didn't come from any historical source, nor did it even come from a piece of music, as a reader may expect given the novel's title and subject. Instead, the seed came from a dream that I had.

The dream became, more or less, the first chapter of the novel: a young woman appearing at the house of composer and virtuoso violinist Antonio Vivaldi, asking him to give her music lessons. It was so vivid and realistic that when I woke up, I couldn't stop thinking about it, couldn't stop wondering about these two people and what their story might be. I also wondered vaguely why I would even have such a dream at all—I knew very little about Vivaldi or Venice—but that was secondary to the tale that was rapidly, insistently unfolding in my head.

So I started writing that very day, because I just had to get the story out. Of course, there was that issue I mentioned above—I knew hardly anything about the place, time period, or historical

~

figure at the center of my fledgling novel. I wanted to do this right, and I knew that in order to do so a lot of serious research would be needed.

I began where any modern writer begins: Google. I had come across the idea, in the historical novel *Vivaldi's Virgins* by Barbara Quick, that opera singer Anna Giró had been Vivaldi's daughter rather than his mistress, the latter being the assumption at the time. In my preliminary Google searching I encountered this idea again on a few websites, and to me it begged the question: if that were true, then who had Anna's mother been? That was the "what if" question I sought to answer with *The Violinist of Venice*.

Since the story would not leave off its clamoring to be told and written down, I did the heavy research work as I wrote. I began with Vivaldi's music. I poked around the iTunes store and downloaded lots of different pieces, both instrumental and vocal, though my focus was violin concertos. Throughout my work on the novel, my collection of Vivaldi's music grew. I listened to so many gorgeous, breathtaking, transcendent pieces of music, and attempted to capture some of them in prose on the pages of the novel. I also tried to blend my imaginings of what the man who had written such music would be like with all the things that history told me of him. This is possibly a flawed method of characterization, but I couldn't resist the impulse to let Vivaldi's greatest legacy—his music—bleed into my portrayal of him as a man.

I also rented a violin, found a local violin teacher, and began taking lessons, which I continued at my college the following semester. I had never so much as touched the instrument when I started writing the novel, and I wanted to have at least a little bit of insight into what my violinist characters experienced. Turns out I am a terrible violinist, but the experience definitely helped inform the novel (and I had a lot of fun!). I was also able to purchase and study some of the scores for pieces mentioned in the novel—it certainly helped, when describing a piece, to have the music right in front of me.

Then, of course, it came time for the hard work—reading *a lot*. I read everything I could find about Vivaldi's life and music, and about Venice. I focused, of course, on 18th-century Venice, but also read histories of the city beginning with its founding. This helped solidify my knowledge of Venice and its history in a way that reading only about my designated time period would not have been able to. Venice is such a unique place, both physically and culturally, and to accurately portray those wild, scandalous, and decadent 18th-century years, I needed to understand how the city and its people had gotten there.

The novel's heroine, Adriana d'Amato, is a fictional character, and this gave me a great deal of freedom in writing. I could have her life take whatever course I chose, and through her explore the aspects of 18th-century Venice that most interested me: the festival of Carnevale, for instance, and the world of the opera theaters. Through her I tried to render the most complete portrait of that time and place I could, in all its beauty and sadness and decay and contradictions.

The last piece of my research puzzle was to actually go to Venice. I had never been there, and I knew that for all my reading and poring over pictures and maps, I could only write about it for so long without seeing it for myself. Not to mention that ever since I was a child, I had been fascinated by this notion of a city that was built in the middle of the water.

Venice is a wonderful place to visit as a historical novelist, as very little has changed about it physically since Vivaldi's day. I was able to learn the layout of the city, learn how people got around there, and see some of the places that appeared in the novel, of course—and when I went home and began the final draft, I even added new locations that I had visited in my travels. Yet more than that, what I took away the most from my visit to Venice—hopefully the first of many—was a vivid awareness of the beauty of the place. There are beautiful views everywhere you turn, a picturesque scene down almost every street. And such beautiful artwork and architecture and music, all created in a city that, realistically, should not exist, but somehow does, through engineering that seems more like magic.

And so in that vein, I wanted to let a sense of beauty permeate the pages of the novel, wanted to make it so that the reader would feel the beauty of Venice from my words, whether they had ever been there or not. Of course, throughout the course of the novel my characters do and experience and endure many things that are not beautiful, even as the city of Venice has always had very real problems and struggles. But through it all, my characters do their best to find the beauty in their lives, in their art, in music. And no matter the time period, the search for beauty has always been a crucial part of the human experience. I hope that, in some small way, my novel can contribute to this search.

~

ALYSSA PALOMBO is a recent graduate of Canisius College, with degrees in English and creative writing. A passionate music lover, she is a classically trained vocalist as well as a big fan of heavy metal. *The Violinist of Venice* is her first novel. She lives in Buffalo, New York. Her website is www.alyssapalombo.com.

ANN PARKER

~

The Silver Rush Mysteries

I was born and raised in California, so I'm a California girl. But my parents, my grandparents, and some of my uncles and aunts are from Colorado. I visited the state a lot as a child and was always drawn to it. At the family reunion in 1997, my Uncle Walt, who has done a lot of family history and genealogy research, happened to mention that my paternal grandmother was raised in Leadville, an old Colorado town set in the heart—and the height—of the Rockies. She loved to tell stories, but I'd never heard her talk about Leadville at all.

"What's Leadville?" I asked. Walt replied, "It was just the biggest silver rush in the world, and a hell-raising town, really fascinating history." By now, I was intrigued. He continued, "I know you want to do some fiction writing. You should research Leadville and set a book there."

Back home, I did some research…and my uncle was right! The more I read about Leadville, the more fascinated I became. The silver rush there hit its peak around 1879, about 30 years after the Gold Rush, which as a California schoolchild I'd learned a lot about (whether I wanted to or not). The town and the region were beautiful, but the Leadville of the Silver Rush was, as my uncle had said, a hell-raising town. Like most boomtowns, it attracted all kinds: people from all over the country and the world, from the credulous to the criminal. There was no way infrastructure or law enforcement could keep up with the huge influx of people thinking they were going to strike it rich at 10,000 feet in the Rockies, where winter lasts nine months out of the year. It felt like the perfect place for fictional exploration.

But what was I going to do with it? What kind of book did I want to write? The path forward became clearer one day when I was talking to my good friend, the mystery writer Camille Minichino. "Ann, you read mysteries all the time. Why don't you make it a mystery?" she asked me.

Though I've been a voracious reader ever since I was a kid and I've always loved mysteries, it had never occurred to me that I could write one. But the idea made sense. At that point I had to go back and look closely at mystery structure, how the books are put together. I had always read them for pleasure: absorbing some of their craft, maybe, but not looking at it with a conscious or analytic eye.

I considered a male protagonist, but decided against that pretty quickly. I had watched a lot of Westerns when I was a child—it was the timeframe of *Have Gun Will Travel, Paladin,* and particularly *The Wild Wild West.* But the thing about the Westerns, which I recognized even when I was young, was that the men had all the fun, all the adventures. Where were the women? They were the wallpaper, the faces in the crowd. That struck me as incredibly unfair. If I was going to write mysteries, I was going to let the girls have some fun, too.

As I was thinking about that, I was reading Dianne Day's Fremont Jones series. Fremont Jones had a spark that I liked. I found myself musing something along the lines of, *Suppose you took the spunkiness of Fremont Jones and turned it darker…wrote someone who took a 'wrong turn' somewhere and who was willing to walk that line between right and wrong, legal and illegal.* From that "what if" I wove my pro-tagonist Inez Stannert, a saloon owner with a complex life and history. I didn't want her perfect, and I didn't want her a spunky young thing. I wanted her to be a woman who'd had some experience in life, and who was willing to compromise her moral standards somewhat when she thought it would help her friends or protect her family. That felt more interesting, and more realistic, too.

It worked to my advantage that women had a lot of opportunity in the 19th-century West. Women entrepreneurs might still get looked on askance, but there was a sense that everyone, not just women, was stepping outside of "normal" or traditional roles. You could change your life, reinvent yourself, start over—often, that's precisely what people were coming to the West to do. They might already have come from Europe to America to try something new. And if that venture didn't work out? You can almost sense them thinking, *All right. We're just going to move a little further West and try again.* I immediately loved that sense of open possibilities.

As I've written the books in what became my Silver Rush series, I've done a lot of research on the silver rush, Colorado, Leadville, and the period generally. Don and Jean Griswold's *History of Leadville and Lake County, Colorado* has been an incredible resource: thousands of pages on Leadville, ordered year by year.

I've also picked up lots of intriguing bits and pieces for the novels, like a magpie. I'll be moving along, I'll notice something, I'll go, *Ooohhh, shiny, I'm going to tuck that aside for later.* One example—which helped inspire my newest novel in the series, *What Gold Buys*—was an email from a very kind woman in England who had a relative or family friend who had come to Leadville hoping to strike it rich during the timeframe of my novels. The poor fellow died in Colorado and was shipped home in a glass coffin. Who wouldn't be fascinated by that?

I still don't know if it was a coffin made entirely of glass. But that got me thinking about what happens when you die far from home, and about death in the 19th-century West generally. My novel before *What Gold Buys*, titled *Mercury's Rise*, had been about tuberculosis, a real scourge at the time. It seemed logical to move from illness to death—how people saw it, what they believed happened afterward. Death was so ever-present in the 19th century. You could step on a nail and die, or perish from what are now totally curable illnesses—people were constantly grieving. So I understand the drive to believe you can connect with someone who is gone that gave rise to the spiritualism movement. Spiritualism is dramatic, rife with fictional possibilities, and women were very prominent within the movement. The characters of fortuneteller and psychic Drina Gizzi and spiritualist Françoise Alexander in *What Gold Buys* grew out of all that.

Drina's daughter Antonia came to life from a similar small detail. I read about a Leadville newspaper giving the boys who sold newspapers in the era handsome new uniforms. That got me thinking about other newsies, children who were part of the period's scenery. Somehow Antonia Gizzi, a young girl who dresses up as a boy to earn money, walked in to my story. She was angry as heck. I found myself asking "Why are you so angry?" and her role developed from there.

As I've written the Silver Rush novels, they've grown to feel more like books in a saga rather than just mysteries—the cast of recurring characters has moved beyond Inez alone, and the world of the books beyond just Leadville. In the end, one of the things that makes me glad I chose to write a mystery series is that allows me to create my own world. I enjoy the puzzle element, but what I love is the way I can make my fictional world behave as I want—sometimes even write in a sense of justice that you don't always get in the real world, in 1879 or today.

~

ANN PARKER earned degrees in Physics and English Literature before falling into a career as a science writer. The only thing more fun for her than slipping oblique Yeats references into a fluid dynamics article is delving into the past. Her Silver Rush historical mystery series is set in the silver boomtown of Leadville, Colorado, in the early 1880s and has been picked as a "Booksellers Favorite" by the Mountains and Plains Independent Booksellers Association. A member of Mystery Writers of America and Women Writing the West, Ann lives with her husband and an uppity cat near Silicon Valley, whence they have weathered numerous high-tech boom-and-bust cycles. Find Ann online at www.annparker.net.

SUE PURKISS

~

Warrior King

*M*ore than any other book I've written, *Warrior King*, which is about Alfred the Great, came about through serendipity. Let me explain. I had previously written three funny middle-grade books about ghosts, witches and the like, and one very different, close-to-the-heart contemporary story, *The Willow Man*. Casting around for my next project, I hit on the idea of a time-travelling dog, who would enable his young master to head back in time to iconic moments in history. The cunning twist was to be that without Matt—the boy—none of these famous incidents would actually have happened.

I decided to start with Alfred and the famous story of how he burnt some cakes while he was masterminding a strategy for defeating the marauding Danes. But I knew very little about him. I hunted out a book I had by Michael Wood about the Dark Ages. I found that Alfred was a fascinating figure: intelligent, curious, and concerned for the well-being of his people. Had he not come through the cake-burning and emerged to defeat the Danes, the English kingdoms would all have become Danish—with what implications for the development of the language, culture and history of the English?

I also discovered—to my delight—that the cake-burning happened on the Isle of Athelney, which is on the Somerset Levels, not far from where I live. I pictured a village devoted to Alfred, just as Tintagel, in Cornwall, is devoted to King Arthur. I imagined shops called *The Burnt Cake-shop* and *Viking Butchers*, and lots of information about my new hero.

What I found was a broad lonely landscape dotted with willows, where birds circled above flooded fields. The Isle itself—actually a low mound that is only sometimes an island—is on private land. I was leaning on a gate gazing up at it when an old man came up and started to chat.

"I expect," he said, "you'll be looking for Alfred."

He wasn't a mind-reader. Alfred was in his thoughts because Athelney was soon to be the subject of a popular TV program called *Time Team*, where a group of investigative archaeologists have three days to uncover hidden mysteries. Suddenly, everything was coming up Alfred.

I was hooked. I forgot about the time-travelling dog, and read all I could about this unusual Dark Age king. I discovered a fascinating figure: a fifth son who could never have been expected to rule; a great fighter and strategist; an intelligent, intensely curious man who learned to read as an adult and went on to write books of his own; an inventor; above all, a ruler who cared not just about power but about his people.

Back to the serendipity. A few months later, I went as an extra pair of hands on a trip with my daughter's class, and happened to overhear the history teacher talking about an open day at Athelney, where Somerset archaeologists would discuss the finds that had been made on the *Time Team* dig.

Of course, I went. They had discovered that Athelney—the name means "Island of the Princes"—had been a high-status site long before Alfred; they had found the remnants of Iron Age palisades, and a good deal of evidence of the abbey that Alfred had built there after his sojourn on the island and subsequent victory over the Danes at the battle of Ethandun (Edington).

And they had found smoke-blackened stones—evidence not of an oven, but of a blacksmith's forge—and a knife of such wondrous workmanship that it could only have been made for a man of very high status.

I felt a shiver down my spine. I was walking in Alfred's footsteps. In this very place, weapons had been forged for use in the crucial battle against the Danes.

I carried on. I visited the sites of significant battles; I tracked on maps the likely route of the journey the young Alfred took with his father to Rome; I read up on the Saxons, on the Vikings, and on Charlemagne, whose descendant Judith (another fascinating character) married Alfred's father when she was little older than Alfred.

And then I read that Bernard Cornwell had beaten me to it. He had already published a novel about Alfred, and I knew very well that anything he had written would fly out of the bookshops, whereas I was an unknown. There seemed no point in going on. My book would languish in a dusty file on my computer. I might as well give up. It's probably what Alfred felt like when he first got to Athelney.

We were about to go for a weekend to stay in a bed and breakfast near Wantage, partly to meet up with friends, and partly to find another battle site nearby. And serendipity struck again. The landlady was the sister of a publisher who had just sent her an early copy of a book by a television historian, David Starkey. He had written a very interesting chapter about Alfred. I told her about the story I had planned, and about Bernard Cornwell. "You have a different story to tell," she said. "You should tell it."

So I did. But when I began to plot it, I ran into another problem. I wanted to write about Alfred's early life as well as about the crucial events of 878, when he would have been 30. But I was a children's writer; this was to be marketed as a children's book. I needed a child for my viewpoint character. The first part would be easy; it would be from Alfred's own point of view. But what about the later part? At first I was stumped.

Then I wondered: How old would his children have been at this stage? And here I hit gold, and the final bit of serendipity. His eldest daughter, Aethelflaed, would have been about nine—perfect! Furthermore, I discovered, she grew up to rule a neighboring country in her own right, becoming the Lady of the Mercians. Clearly, she was a girl of some character.

In fact, her story was so fascinating that I almost wanted to abandon Alfred and write about her instead. I didn't. *Warrior King* was about both of them. But I had the chance to revisit her later, when I wrote a story about her in an anthology created by the writers of The History Girl blog and called *The Daughters of Time*.

Aethelflaed had a daughter called Aelfwyn. And there is a mystery surrounding her fate—she disappeared, and it's not known what became of her. Perhaps one day, I'll write about her, too...

SUE PURKISS has published three books for young readers; a contemporary novel, *The Willow Man*; and two historical novels. The first of these, *Warrior King*, is a re-imagining of the story of Alfred the Great, partly told through the eyes of his daughter. *Emily's Surprising Voyage*, Sue's most recent book, is again for younger readers, and is set on Brunel's beautiful ship, the SS Great Britain. Sue's story about Alfred the Great's daughter Aethelflaed appears in *The Daughters of Time*, an anthology of stories by the authors of The History Girls blog. Find Sue online at www.suepurkiss.blogspot.co.uk and www.the-history-girls.blogspot.com.

CELIA REES

Witch Child and Sorceress

W here do ideas come from? That is the enduring mystery and magic of writing fiction. I had the initial idea for *Witch Child* and *Sorceress* when I was researching a completely different book, a YA novel with a heavy dose of the supernatural. I was looking for a conjurer, a magician, on whom to base my villain, when I came across an account of Matthew Hopkins, self-appointed Witch Finder General, who operated in England in the Civil War Period (1642-1651). For 20 shillings he would rid a town of witches. He always earned his fee.

I began to think: what did it *mean* to be a witch? Those accused were generally women: poor, single, old, without male protection. They were often healers and midwives. Those who could not afford doctors—that is, most people—depended on them. But their skill was dangerous. Those who cure can kill. What if archaeologist-folklorist Margaret Murray's theory, that witchcraft was some kind of pagan cult survival, was correct? The knowledge could be passed down through the female line. Then my thoughts took a leaping arc of inspiration. This would make it a shamanistic religion. Where else in the world was shamanism practiced? North America.

A memory surfaced from the deep past: a university seminar reading Nathaniel Hawthorne's *Ethan Brand*, a description of limekiln burners, their kiln the only spark of light in dark forests that stretched for hundreds, thousands of miles. I remember thinking how frightening it must have been for those first settlers, surrounded by impenetrable darkness on the edge of a vast, unknown continent.

A story was forming. It fitted the history. Matthew Hopkins's rampage marked the last outbreak of witch persecution in England. America was home to a shamanistic people. English settlers took the deadly spores of fear and superstition with them, to grow and bloom fed by the terrifying darkness all around them. How do we know that? Because of Salem, of course.

I began to think: What if there was a British girl who lives with her grandmother, a healer, who is teaching her the skills? A Witch Finder comes to the village and "healer" is suddenly "witch." The grandmother? Accused and hanged. The girl? On her own. If there were a cult, others would look after her. She could be taken to America where she would be would be caught between two cultures. One would want to hang her; the other would revere her for her power….

I knew I had a book. But the story of the book is not just the story of the idea. I had to sell it. My publishers were not interested in historical fiction for teenagers. I put the idea away. Then, by a supreme piece of serendipity, I found a publisher. Sarah Odedina, an editor at Bloomsbury, was driving back to London from Scotland when she saw a memorial to women burned as witches. She began to think, what if there was a *girl* who was a witch? Sarah contacted my agent wondering if she knew anyone who might be interested in writing something along these lines. My agent called me thinking it might appeal to me. I hauled out my synopsis and couple of chapters and sent them off to Bloomsbury. Sarah called me back immediately. It was so exactly what she was looking for that it seemed like magic.

I had a publisher. Now the book had to be written. Could I do it? I'd never written a purely historical novel before. I had to find my own way of working. First, I had to be sure that the story could work historically. Yon can't change, bend or break historical fact. Nothing destroys the *mise-en-scène* of a historical novel more completely than anachronism or factual inaccuracy. Writers of historical fiction face a double challenge. The facts have to fit on the historical level and the level of story. Research is about finding out what is possible, but we are not historians. Our task is not just about accuracy. We are looking for those kernels of real experience that will add spark and fire, cast the flaring light of insight into the lost, dark hinterland of the past, illuminate our characters, and help to make them into real, dynamic people living in a specific time—to make history come alive.

Sarah wanted to split the story in two. The first book (*Witch Child*) would be a diary, written by the main character, Mary. Names are important, especially in historical fiction. At time of extreme religious dissension, Mary had a universality respected by all Christian denominations. I chose a diary because the form binds the reader close to the protagonist. If my other editors were right and teens weren't that interested in history, a diary might be a way of overcoming that diffidence. But I was immediately presented with a problem of my own making. The diary had to be secret. Mary had to hide it. But where?

Research is not just reading. It's also going to places, being open, aware, receptive. On a visit the American Museum in Bath, in the Quilt and Textiles Room, I read that early colonial quilts were often stuffed with rags and *paper!* Mary could sew her diary into a quilt. Quilting was more than a solution to my logistical problem. Searchers after seditious materials would be men; quilting was women's work, beneath their notice. Moreover, quilting was women's *art*, their means of creative self-expression in a male dominated society. The quilt idea opened realms of possibilities. If the diary was hidden, it could be found. The found document is a device as old as the novel and as new as *The Blair Witch Project*, which was showing at the time. I watched the film and wondered: what if the diary was discovered, its pages pieced together and published? Not only would that give the diary the veracity of the found document, it would link *Witch Child* to the second book, *Sorceress*.

I always knew that Mary would leave her colonial settlement and join Native Americans. But which people, and how to tell the story? There could be no diaries in the wilderness. I had to find another device. The Native Americans held the answer. Shamanistic practice had been part of my first inspiration. Mary's story could be discovered by a descendant, a young Native American woman, with the help of an aunt who was a medicine woman. This would give the whole work a satisfying symmetry. I just had to tell it with sensitivity and accuracy.

Luck and synchronicity always have their part to play. When *Witch Child* had been taken up by Candlewick Press in America, I was invited to a publisher sales conference in Cambridge, Massachusetts. At a party, someone told me about the Six Nations Indian Museum, located in Onchiota, in the Appalachian region of New York State. I knew I had to go there. The keeper of the museum, John Fadden, a member of the Mohawk Nation, agreed to act as my consultant. Finally, I was ready to write *Sorceress*.

~

CELIA REES has written over 20 books in different genres but is perhaps best known for her historical fiction. Her first historical novel, *Witch Child*, was translated into 28 languages. *Witch Child* and subsequent titles, *Sorceress* and *Pirates!*, were shortlisted for the Guardian, Whitbread (Costa) and W.H. Smith Awards in the UK and won awards in the UK, USA, France and Italy. Her latest book, the dark contemporary thriller *This is Not Forgiveness*, was nominated for several UK awards and was one of *Kirkus Reviews'* Best Teen Books of 2012. She lives in Leamington Spa and divides her time between writing, talking to readers in schools and libraries, and reviewing and teaching creative writing. Find her at www.celiarees.com and www.the-history-girls.blogspot.com.

ELIZABETH ROSNER

Electric City

I
come from Electric City.
For a long time, this was the first line of my novel, and
even after I had switched to third person and therefore
could no longer use this sentence, it haunted me like a stubborn and
relentless piece of music. The truth is that the creation of this book
began the moment I realized I hadn't yet written about where I come
from. I've written about Berkeley, where I live now and have lived
for nearly 30 years. I've written about places in Europe where I've
traveled and where my parents came from. But aside from a few
poems, the deep dive into exploring the place where I was born and
raised was something I'd been avoiding, perhaps because it was a
place I was so glad to have escaped, and a place that for many reasons
never quite felt entirely like home.

About eight years ago, I was sitting in the audience listening to a
lecture given by James Houston at the Squaw Valley Community
of Writers. He was talking about the importance of setting, the

importance of PLACE, and I felt the top of my head cracking open. *Schenectady!* I thought. The place I left behind at the age of 16, traveling as far from home as I could get without leaving the planet. The place I continued to reject, during decades of visiting my parents who had remained there. The place I both knew and didn't know. So maybe it was time.

As soon as I found out that one of the oldest nicknames for Schenectady was "Electric City," the title of the book felt chiseled into stone. For a few years, the title was my favorite thing about the book, especially during the stretches when I felt the work-in-progress was a disaster. I loved saying the title out loud when people asked me what I was working on, and I loved seeing the looks on their faces when they heard the phrase. Every once in a while, someone would want to know more, at least a little bit more, and I would explain that it was about my hometown. "Home of General Electric," I'd say. And they would say, "Ah." As if they knew.

As it soon became clear, there was an astonishing (to me) and complicated history for my birthplace, much richer and more intriguing than I could have imagined. During an early-in-the-process phone conversation with my father, who seemed tickled by the idea that I was writing about Schenectady, he said, "Why don't you write about Charles Steinmetz." "Who?" I asked. "Look him up," my father said. "You'll see."

I was intending at that point to open the novel on the day of the Great Northeast Blackout of 1965, an event I could only vaguely recall because I was five years old at the time. I'd decided that my main character (my first-person narrator, originally), was going to be 15 years old, so that her memories of the blackout would be vivid and significant. I gave her my own birthday of New Year's Eve, except instead of being born on the last day of the 1950s, she would be born on the last day of the 1940s. I gave her the name Sophie Levine. And then I started reading about Charles Proteus Steinmetz.

Many novelists find that when they're doing research for a book, nearly everything around them seems to conspire in the direction of the story—that is, the world of "coincidence" and "synchronicity" starts offering up perfect details and data for your use. When I read that Steinmetz was a dwarf and a hunchback, that he was almost turned away from Ellis Island for being deformed and sickly, that he floated up and down the Mohawk River in a canoe that he used as his office, that he wore a coonskin cap and smoked cigars—everything I learned about him seemed perfectly designed for a wonderfully eccentric, compelling fictional character.

And yet, I had plenty of inventing to do. I became as fascinated with what I could find out about him as I was intrigued by what I could not find out. I held imaginary dialogues with him inside my head, filling in the spaces between the so-called facts of his life.

As a writer who often works in fragments, following character and image more than plot, I am frequently in a state of "blindness" when it comes to the architecture of my fiction. I am fond of quoting E.L. Doctorow, who famously said that writing a novel is "like driving in tule fog. All you need to do is see a few feet in front of you, and you can drive all the way across the country like that."

By chance, I met Doctorow while I was grappling with that state of writing in the dark, and in particular I wanted to ask him how he managed to handle real-life characters with so much grace and originality. I'd been worrying over the "real" Steinmetz and how to take liberties with his personality, his life. Doctorow said, "I just treat them the way I treat my other characters. Think of it like being a portrait painter—you're not necessarily aiming for pure realism but for an interpretation of the person sitting in front of you." That was the reassurance I needed to keep moving forward a few more feet at a time.

Some of my most exciting discoveries happened when I closed my eyes and remembered my own childhood, scenes from that hometown I had always been so eager to leave behind. I wouldn't be the first writer to be inspired by the emotional and geographical and temporal distance between me and my birthplace, realizing that I could only feel inspired by home once I had been away from it for many, many years.

"You can't go home again" was one of the many clichés I held in mind as I wrote. "Home is where the heart is. Home is the place where, when you go back, they have to take you in. Home is where I want to be." But my hometown was where I *didn't* want to be. Except in my imagination, and except for the loves and losses of my characters, with whom I traveled on both literal and metaphoric journeys toward and away from themselves, from their birthplaces, and from one another. Writing (and completing!) *Electric City* transported me back into my childhood, allowed me to revisit my adolescence and young adulthood—until I reached the time in which I left behind my hometown for good. I learned, along with my characters, a truth both personal and universal: If we are lucky, we get to discover that home is the place we carry inside ourselves.

$\sim$

ELIZABETH ROSNER is a novelist, poet, and essayist living in Berkeley, California. Her third novel, *Electric City*, was named among the best books of 2014 by National Public Radio. Her acclaimed poetry collection, *Gravity*, was also published in 2014. *The Speed of Light*, Rosner's 2001 debut novel, was translated into nine languages. Short-listed for the Prix Femina, the book won several literary prizes in both the US and Europe, including the Prix France Bleu Gironde; the Great Lakes Colleges Award for New Fiction; and Hadassah Magazine's Ribalow Prize, judged by Elie Wiesel. *Blue Nude*, Rosner's second novel, was selected as one of the *San Francisco Chronicle's* best books of 2006. Her essays, poems and book reviews are widely published in leading periodicals. Find out more at www.elizabethrosner.com.

STEVEN SAYLOR

~

The Roma Sub Rosa® Novels

*I*n one of his book review columns in *Ellery Queen's Mystery Magazine*, Jon L. Breen noted: "Historical detective novels have become so popular and plentiful that eventually there may be no historical event of significance without a fictional mystery grafted on to it."

That may be stretching it a bit, but I can vouch, both as a reader and writer, for the allure of mixing history and detection.

When I was in high school I craved the exotic and remote locales of science fiction and fantasy. As I got older, suspending my disbelief got a bit tougher, I suppose, and those genres worked for me less and less. Still, I craved that all-enveloping satisfaction of escaping to another time and place, and I started seeking it in historical fiction; the only problem is that really good historical novels are few and far between. In my late twenties I discovered Le Carré, and found a similar satisfaction in exploring his minutely detailed and morally vexing fictive landscape; but once I'd read everything from *The Spy*

Who Came in From the Cold to *The Little Drummer Girl*, plus Graham Greene and Joseph Conrad, the espionage genre ran dry for me; good spy novels are as hard to find as good historical novels. It wasn't until I reached thirty or so that I discovered and devoured Sherlock Holmes and thereafter plunged head-first into the world of the detective mystery. The allure of the puzzle, the cozy setting, the charm of the sleuth all captivated me. (After Holmes, Stuart Palmer's Hildegarde Withers stories are my absolute favorites.)

Still, I had a hankering for something more expansive and escapist—the large-scale world-creation that I'd last found in historical novels like those of Mary Renault and Robert Graves. For me, the idea of historical mystery as the perfect literary form came together when I read Umberto Eco's *The Name of the Rose*, one of those rare books, like *The Lord of the Rings* or *Wuthering Heights*, that resonated to my core. It was superb historical fiction, rigorously intellectual and yet evocatively sensual, transporting me to a distant time and place; and it was also a mind-bending mystery, presenting puzzles practical, poetical and metaphysical, with a wise sleuth to accompany me through the labyrinth (or in this case, the library/ maze). What combination could be more satisfying?

I explored the historical mysteries of Ellis Peters, and found a tiny treasure-trove in the Dr. Sam Johnson short stories of Lillian de la Torre. But what I really craved was a full-scale historical mystery set in ancient Rome, my favorite period since childhood, when Hollywood epics and Classics Illustrated comics introduced me to the larger-than-life dramas of Caesar and Cleopatra and their contemporaries. At the time, such a novel didn't seem to exist, so I figured I'd simply have to write it myself.

The direct inspiration for the first novel in my Roma Sub Rosa®
series came from a trip to Rome. Having explored the ancient Forum
and wandered though the ruins of Ostia, I felt a craving for a taste
of ancient Roman literature, a field I knew from studying ancient
history and Classics at the University of Texas at Austin. Back home
in San Francisco, I spotted a copy of the Penguin edition of Cicero's
Murder Trials (translated by Michael Grant) in a used book store,
took it home, and settled down to read his oration "In Defense of
Sextus Roscius."

The rest is history—and mystery. Reading between the lines of
the scandalous murder case that launched Cicero's career, I caught
a glimmer of what I thought would be a terrific detective story. I
started digging, plotting, writing—historical research is delightful
detective work—and two years later, *Roman Blood* was finished. In
the fall of 1991 it was published by St. Martin's Press. The first
printing was small, and the second even smaller, but the very fact
that there was a second printing prompted my editor, Michael
Denneny, to press me for a sequel. *Arms of Nemesis*, set against the
background of the Spartacus slave revolt, followed in 1992.

As of 2016, the Roma Sub Rosa® series featuring my sleuth,
Gordianus the Finder, runs to 13 novels and two collections of short
stories.

(In between novels I stay busy writing a related series of short
stories, also featuring Gordianus, often published in Ellery Queen's
Mystery Magazine. The first story in the series, "A Will Is a Way,"
won the 1993 Robert L. Fish Memorial Award from the Mystery
Writers of America, given to the best debut short story in the genre.)

When I started *Roman Blood*, I thought I was working on a fairly lonely patch of literary ground. It wasn't until I had finished the manuscript that I saw Colleen McCullough's epic *First Man in Rome* in a bookstore. Well, I figured, as I watched it leap onto the best seller lists, anything that gets readers interested in ancient Rome can only help. Then came Lindsay Davis' *Silver Pigs* and John Maddox Roberts' *SPQR*, both of which have turned into series. Then I discovered a couple of Roman mysteries that had been published in 1989, *A Roman Death* by Australian Joan O'Hagan, and *Dogheaded Death* by Ray Faraday Nelson. And when *Roman Blood* came out, my own publisher had yet another Roman mystery in the very same catalogue, *Roman Nights* by Ron Burns!

It's curious that all these mysteries with Roman settings came out so close together. Given the timeframe, it's clear that none of the writers involved took inspiration from the others. It was just a curious coincidence that we all experienced a similar brain wave at roughly the same time.

I only hope that readers will continue to pick up on that brain wave, and that the market for detective historicals continues to flourish and grow, so that I can keep taking my own time-trips back to ancient Rome with Gordianus the Finder in search of murder, mayhem, and clues. Anyone out there with a taste for historical sleuthing is more than welcome to come along.

STEVEN SAYLOR is the author of the Roma Sub Rosa® series of historical mysteries featuring Gordianus the Finder and set in the ancient Rome of Cicero, Caesar, and Cleopatra. The latest novels in the series—*The Seven Wonders, Raiders of the Nile,* and *Wrath of the Furies*—are prequels about Gordianus in his youth. Steven is also the author of two novels set in his native Texas and the international bestsellers *Roma: The Novel of Ancient Rome* and *Empire: The Novel of Imperial Rome,* two novels comprising a multi-generational saga that spans the first 1200 years of the city. A third novel in this series is currently in the research stage. He divides his time between homes in Berkeley, California, and Austin, Texas. Find Steven online at www.stevensaylor.com.

SOPHIE SCHILLER

Transfer Day

hile I was growing up in St. Thomas, a former Danish colony in the West Indies, a single nagging question would return time and time again: Why are there no books detailing the rich, vibrant history of the Danish West Indies? After all, the islands have been praised for their beauty for centuries; the capital, Charlotte Amalie, possesses one of the most picturesque natural harbors in the world. For inspiration, all a writer would have to do is gaze at her lush green hills, abundant tropical flowers, quaint Danish colonial architecture, and sandy white beaches bordered by turquoise water, not to mention those ubiquitous red-roofed houses that dot her hillsides.

Sometimes on Fridays before sunset, I would wander down to the waterfront and sit on a bench, watching the *Dannebrog* being lowered up on Denmark Hill and letting my mind drift off. As the sun inched closer to the horizon, I always left feeling despondent, wanting more. Somewhere along the way, I decided that I would write my own novel about this place.

For 250 years the islands of St. Thomas, St. John, and St. Croix were collectively known as the Danish West Indies. By the 1860s the Danes desired to unload their tropical island colony and turned to the United States for help. But it wasn't until World War I, with the threat of German encroachment in the New World, that the United States completed negotiations and a treaty was pushed through both the American Congress and the Danish *Rigsdag*. During the height of the German Kaiser's submarine campaign against the Allies, the islands were quickly sold and transferred to the US for $25 million in gold bullion.

Until now, this amazing event in history had never been fully tackled in either fiction or nonfiction. In my mind, this story presented fertile ground for suspense, drama, and conflict. After all, it's not every day that a territory is handed over from one world power to another. I wondered what changes the islands inhabitants were going through and about their individual stories.

Located high on a steep hill behind the town is one of the oldest surviving Sephardic synagogues in the Western Hemisphere, a cultural relic of a bygone era when tall sailing ships ruled the waves. Since St. Thomas once boasted a prominent Sephardic Jewish population, I decided to tell the story through the eyes of a Sephardic girl from this community. Sephardic Jews played an important role in expanding Denmark's trading ambitions in spices, sugar, tobacco, rum, cotton, indigo, ginger, cacao and coffee. However, due to series of natural disasters including a hurricane in 1867, the islands began a rapid decline, causing many young men to grow frustrated and search for new and more prosperous lands. The result was a large number of young women at the beginning of the 20th century who faced the real prospect of a lifetime of spinsterhood. It is under these conditions that I introduce my main character, Abigail Maduro, who is facing an uncertain future on a male-depleted island during a time of war, when the future of the world is at stake.

Now that I had found my main character, I needed to introduce the element of danger. From scouring old *New York Times* articles, I knew that an important office of the Hamburg-America Steamship Line (HAPAG) was located on St. Thomas. Thoughts swirled in my mind over what went on in this operation. Who was running it? Were they only engaged in maritime activities, as they claimed, or were they also involved in more secretive pursuits?

I approached a Danish contact of mine. To my great fortune he put me in touch with a close friend of his from Germany whose grandfather, Julius Jochimsen, had been the Director of the HAPAG office in St. Thomas, as well as serving as German Consul for the Danish West Indies. In August of 2008, I flew to Washington, D.C. to have a look in the National Archives about any information they had on him—and I knew I had struck gold.

The picture that emerged was a dramatic one. I found out that even in this quiet Danish island enclave, the German captains, officers and engineers were all reserves in the *Kaiserliche Marine*, the Imperial German Navy. Upper management in the steamship office maintained close contact with Berlin via coded radio transmissions over a *Telefunken* wireless radio station hidden in at least one of their steamships, and through another one in the island of Puerto Rico. Other documents I uncovered showed heated confrontations between HAPAG steamers presumed to be carrying war contraband and American Customs officials in San Juan, Puerto Rico—confrontations that resulted in cannon fire, seizures, and imprisonment. But the greatest discovery of all was that the German Consul was also the Head of the HAPAG office and in all likelihood a member of the ultra-secretive *Ettapendienst*, a secret German naval supply system that existed all around the globe. Confirming my suspicions, I found that one week after the US declared war against Germany, this director, along with all his German colleagues, was arrested and shipped to a US prisoner of war camp. This was fascinating stuff! But how would I turn it into a novel?

Julius Adolph Jochimsen is a heretofore-unknown historical figure whose colorful life is worth describing. Family pictures show a handsome, confident man with piercing blue eyes, tailored suits, and a firm, resolute look. Cleverly, Jochimsen left behind few clues as to the exact nature of his activities on St. Thomas. Years later, he would relate that he had three distinct jobs upon the outbreak of World War I. In addition to his roles as German consul and director of the HAPAG office, he was involved in something he referred to as "B.E./V.M." Subsequent research suggests that B.E. stands for *Bevollmächtigter der Etappe*, which means an assigned agent of the *Etappendienst*, Germany's secret intelligence-gathering and logistics service that supplied German warships, raiders and U-boats from neutral ports around the world with coal, money, provisions, and even ships. The "V.M." portion probably stands for *Vertrauensmann*, which literally means "confidence man." These were discreet, confident, reliable German nationals who were used for naval military purposes. I believe that when Jochimsen signed his name with the initials

"B.E./V.M.", he was leaving behind credible evidence that he was, indeed, an intelligence officer of the *Etappendienst*.

Julius Jochimsen inspired my novel's Lothar Langsdorff. I then began to consider the possibility of introducing a U-boat captain character in my novel. My fictional Erich Seibold deserts the war because he refuses to sink any more passenger ships. Using his wits, he talks his way aboard a tramp steamer headed to the West Indies where he decides to hide out on a nice, quiet, neutral Danish island. Once there, he is aided by a local girl, Abigail Maduro, who gives him shelter in the basement of her spinster aunt's house. Ultimately, Erich reveals the truth about his situation, but unbeknownst to him, he's being watched. Langsdorff, the German Consul, discovers his true identity and blackmails him into serving the Fatherland. Langsdorff's overriding ambition is to orchestrate a German takeover of the islands so he can be installed as their first German governor. Later, after the islands are transferred to the United States, Seibold is in even hotter water. He's no longer just a German war deserter: he's now a German soldier trapped behind enemy lines who has morphed into a wanted German spy.

Once I had my three main characters, the story flowed naturally. Throw in a few local West Indian characters, a sympathetic Danish judge, and the US Marines, and a rousing, fast-paced thriller emerged. Once I connected with my characters, I let them tell the story in their own words. In the end, I believe a certain magic was created, the magic of bringing the past to life.

SOPHIE SCHILLER was born in Paterson, NJ and grew up in the West Indies. Among other oddities her family tree contains a Nobel prize-winning physicist and a French pop singer. She loves stories that carry the reader back in time to exotic and far-flung locations. She was educated at American University in Washington, DC and lives in Brooklyn. In addition to *Transfer Day*, she is the author of *Race to Tibet*, a high-altitude adventure and survival story set in the world's most forbidden country. She is currently working on *Island of Eternal Fire*, a historical thriller set in Martinique during the deadliest volcanic disaster of the 20th century. Find out more about Sophie and her work online at www.sophieschiller.blogspot.com.

CAM TERWILLIGER

~

Yet Wilderness Grew in My Heart

ince I arrived in Montréal, I've been doing research for a novel called *Yet Wilderness Grew in My Heart*, a book set in 1757 during the French and Indian War. In a nutshell, it explores the panoply of cultures that clashed and combined in northeastern North America, giving birth to the bustling, cosmopolitan region we take for granted today. After months of work, I've found the picture to be even more complex than I suspected, involving dozens of native peoples, English, French, and Dutch colonists, as well as a flood of enslaved Africans and indentured servants from Scotland, Ireland, and Germany. Of all these groups, however, it's been especially thought-provoking to study the Mohawk people, the eastern member of the Iroquois Confederacy, an alliance of six indigenous nations that originated in New York's Mohawk Valley, the corridor where I-90 runs now.

To learn more about the Mohawks, I take a bus across the Saint Lawrence River every Tuesday to visit the reservation of Kahnawà:ke,

~

a community of 8,000 Mohawks located across the water from Montréal. Composed of two-lane roads lined by modest houses and stores, Kahnawà:ke appears like most small towns until you notice that the stop signs feature the Mohawk word for stop: "testan." After another moment of looking, you'll notice many houses and cars fly a distinct purple flag. Featuring a white pine tree flanked by two rectangles to either side, this is the flag of the Iroquois Confederacy, which still unites the modern communities of the Iroquois, found predominantly in New York, Québec, and Ontario.

Near the town center of Kahnawà:ke, you'll find one of the epicenters of traditional Mohawk culture: Kanien'kehá:ka Onkwawén:na Raotitióhkwa Language and Cultural Center. This is where I spend my day, researching in the library and asking the patient staff countless questions. When I first arrived here, I was craving nuts-and-bolts information about Mohawks during the colonial era to make my novel more concrete and historically accurate. I wanted to know: What did they eat? Wear? What did their houses look like? And though I've learned a good deal about these things, something else became clear as well: the misalignment between native history and the depiction of native history by contemporary media.

During the flood of Westerns that typified the early and mid-20th century, native people almost always played the villains—bloodthirsty barbarians who terrorized innocent white settlers. It's a relief that this stereotype has fallen by the wayside in recent decades; however that doesn't mean natives are always rendered with the complexity they deserve. Many films and novels continue to paint historical natives as noble savages, simplistic people who were doomed to extinction by "progress": the advanced technologies and societies brought by Euro-American colonists. Essentially, natives are mis-represented as childlike innocents, and it's due to this "purity" that they are victimized by the complicated and corrupt world of modern "civilization," a world beyond their understanding.

This romantic yet extremely patronizing view was popularized by James Fenimore Cooper in the 19th century with his Leather-stocking novels (the most famous being *The Last of the Mohicans*). Yet nearly two centuries later, contemporary films espouse the same gauzy mix of idealization and condescension, notable examples being *Dances with Wolves* and Disney's recent relaunch of *The Lone Ranger*. In a form of what anthropologist Renato Rosaldo calls "imperialist nostalgia," these films elegize traditional native societies as the relics of humanity's quaint and primitive past, rather than treating native societies as the true equal of European ones.

The history of the Mohawks and their allies in the Iroquois Confederacy runs completely counter to this harmful depiction. Rather than being guileless primitives, the Mohawks proved to be very shrewd at negotiating the political order created by European imperialism. Trapped between French Canada and the American colonies, the Mohawks found themselves in a dire situation in the 1600s. However, their highly developed government and its strategic approach to diplomacy allowed them to turn this position to their advantage. As tensions between French and English colonists grew, the Mohawks played these rival empires against one another, savvily creating the political agency they needed to protect their people.

Everyone knew that whatever empire the Iroquois Confederacy allied with would certainly win if war broke out between France and England in North America. Since the Mohawks held a strong voice in the council procedures of the Confederacy government, this meant that both France and England were continuously courting their favor. However, rather than accepting offers of alliance out of hand, the Mohawks used their position to negotiate. When sending diplomats to the French, they subtly (and sometimes blatantly) insinuated they might ally with England if treated poorly. When sending diplomats to the English, they suggested the opposite. In the end, the Confederacy would decide to remain neutral in 1701 at a meeting called the "Great Peace of Montréal." This decision actually resulted in preferential treatment from both empires in the form of trade relationships and promises not to interfere with Confederacy business. It was an insightful foreign policy strategy that kept the Mohawks and their allies in a place of power for over a century after their first contact with Europeans in the early 1600s. It was only the outbreak of the French and Indian War in 1753 that finally upset the balance they engineered.

This is just one of many stories that gives the lie to current day fictionalizations that depict natives as Edenic people suddenly pushed to extinction by the arrival of European civilizations outside their comprehension. Native people had a sophisticated web of cultures and governments before Europeans arrived. And after Europeans arrived, they were highly capable of adapting to the circumstances brought by each new century. To leave these things out of our film and fiction only creates plots where native people are denied narrative agency. Despite the many hardships inflicted on them, indigenous nations were never simply victims.

From the privileged standpoint of a white American, it's not my place to speak for native people like the Mohawks. But I do hope new representations of the past both by natives and non-natives will allow us to reevaluate our shared history, replacing two-dimensional characters with ones that are at once more accurate, more interesting, and more complex. As all writers know, it's never too late to reinvent our stories.

CAM TERWILLIGER's fiction and narrative journalism can be found online in *American Short Fiction, Electric Literature, The Rumpus,* and *Narrative,* the latter of which named him one of "15 Under 30." In print, his writing appears in *West Branch, Post Road,* and *Gettysburg Review,* among others. His work has been supported by fellowships and scholarships from the Fulbright Program, the James Jones First Novel Fellowship, and the Massachusetts Cultural Council, the Virginia Center for Creative Arts, and to the Bread Loaf, Tin House, and Sewanee Writers' Conferences. He teaches at Drew University and lives in Brooklyn, New York. Find him online at www.camterwilliger.com.

JANET TODD

~

A Man of Genius

I began my novel with this passage to introduce my main character, Ann, through what was in her head: the kind of work she wrote and read:

> Annabelle looked at the corpse. Hands and head separate. Blood had leaked from wrists and neck. Fluid covered part of the distorted features. The open eyes were stained so that they glared through their own darkness. A smell of rotting meat.
>
> He'd come silently into the room and read from behind her. He smiled.
>
> Ann felt the smile. "I will cross out the fluid and rotting meat," she said without looking up.

She'd been writing Gothic novels for many years and her own and other people's plots had filled her imagination from childhood to the present day (the early 1820s). Yet, when faced with a Gothic world of torment and pursuit, she was as bewildered as anyone else would have been—and as any of the heroines of the novels she read and invented.

My purpose in *A Man of Genius* is to bring together a woman writer who sees herself as a jobbing novelist and a male poet who's regarded by many as a "genius." The exhilaration and pain of their relationship come from a combination of fascination and repulsion on both sides. She may suffer more severely, but the relationship is, at base, one of mutual torment. However, the work is a psychological and historical mystery and nothing is ever quite what it seems at first....

For my work as a critic and biographer of women in the late 18th and early 19th centuries, I read a lot of Gothic novels. I relished the gory woodcuts that often accompanied their title pages. Wonderfully crude and energetic.

I was especially interested in the women who wrote them. The authors weren't all women but a substantial number clearly were. On the whole their lives are obscure, but when we can hear them at all, they make no claims for their hackwork and are eager to state they are not encroaching on the male territory of Literature. Often they claim they write only for money and because they have to: they are spinsters with ailing fathers, or they are widows or abandoned wives.

While the mass market was growing for cheap novels and sensational tales, fed by scribbling writers, a contrasting cult of the "genius" grew up. He—and it was usually a "he"—was understood to be a distinctive and specially endowed human being. Consequently, he was not constrained by the same morality and rules as other mortals.

To sustain his role he needed immense self-confidence as well as the belief, even adulation, of others.

My biography, *Death and the Maidens*, described the effect of a real and haunted "genius"—the poet Percy Bysshe Shelley—on Fanny, the eldest daughter of the great feminist writer Mary Wollstonecraft, as well as on her half sister Mary Shelley, whom he later married, and on his first wife, Harriet. In *A Man of Genius*, an entirely fictional work, I imagine what occurs when the assumed genius begins to doubt his superior powers and when his lover fears her idol might have no substance.

The setting for much of *A Man of Genius* is Venice. I describe the city at a special moment in its history. For centuries Venice had grown rich and powerful as the dominant maritime and commercial state along the Adriatic. It boasted a thousand-year-old past as an independent republic. It had been home to the greatest sculptors and architects, as well as to the most celebrated Renaissance painters: Tintoretto, Veronese and Titian. Its richness in money and art was legendary.

But, by the end of the 18th century, it had suffered a long decline, and the French emperor Napoleon Bonaparte found little opposition in 1797 when he decided to conquer it and subsume it into his Italian empire.

After this shaming defeat, control of Venice was shunted back and forwards between France and Austria until after the battle of Waterloo and the final defeat of Napoleon, when it fell finally into Austrian hands and was made part of the kingdom of Lombardy and Venetia. A few Venetians collaborated with the Austrian masters, appreciating some aspects of the order they brought to the city.

Others preferred the French as being closer to them in temperament, though more plundering of Venetian treasures. Others hugely resented what had happened to Venice and plotted for independence— an independence that would never return. In 1866 Venice was subsumed into the new kingdom of Italy.

The run down and conquered city of 1819 and 1820 is the backdrop of my story. Venice was still at that time part of the Grand Tour for gentlemen from Britain, for it retained much of its amazing art and architecture. At the same time it was beginning to attract more modest middle-class tourists. These were armed with an increasing array of guidebooks.

The era of mass tourism was, however, still in the future. It awaited the coming of the railway.

One of the more bizarre events happening at the time my characters travelled to Venice was the scandal of the British royal family. As so often in history, the royals provided much entertainment for the public at home and abroad. To secure the succession, the dissolute Prince Regent had been urged into an alliance with a German princess, Caroline of Brunswick. He took an instant dislike to her and desperately sought a way out of the hated marriage. Over the next years, as she travelled with a rather *louche* entourage around Europe, he worked to establish enough evidence to bring about a divorce. She was especially linked in scandal with an obscure Italian called Bartolomeo Pergami, much decorated with the honors she bestowed on him: the pair provided great amusement through the newspapers and cartoons. My characters in Venice couldn't avoid hearing of what was entertaining all of Europe.

So my novel is set in specific history but is not about history. It occurs in a particular place that is both real and imaginary. But then, there is always something "imaginary" about Venice.

~

JANET TODD has worked as an academic in Ghana, Puerto Rico, the US, Scotland, India and England. Until recently, she was President of Lucy Cavendish College, University of Cambridge, where she established the Lucy Cavendish Fiction Prize. She has been a critic and editor as well as a biographer of Jane Austen, Aphra Behn (in a biography shortly to be reissued), and Mary Wollstonecraft and her daughters. Recently she has become a novelist with two works, *A Man of Genius*, set in Venice and Regency London, and *Lady Susan Plays the Game*, a spinoff from a Jane Austen novella. Her website is www.janettodd.co.uk.

BOB VAN LAERHOVEN

~

The Shadow of The Mole

*A*popular question in the interviews I give is, "Why do you write historical fiction?" First, I answer that I only write historical fiction now and then. Second, I elaborate on the diverse literary possibilities historical fiction offers. Of all those possibilities, I like most real historical characters in imagined situations; fictional characters in documented historical situations; and fictional characters in fictional situations, yet in the context of a real historical period.

It amuses me to call myself an "historical swindler." Historical fiction—and to some extent even the science of history —is, after all, a "fraud." Herodotus of Hallicarnassus, often called the father of historiography, already admitted that historians wrote "more and less reliably" about the past, depending on their "intelligence and temperament." Human brains are wired to experience reality as mixed with fiction, and to interpret fiction as interwoven with reality. Even if we want it desperately, for humankind the truth remains a chimera. Nietzsche has put it down elegantly: "Truths are illusions about which one has forgotten that this is what they are."

I also used to answer with some evasive quip when the "why" question arose, for I really didn't know why I sometimes write historical novels. However, while writing this short essay, I think I have discovered the reason. From the more than 30 books I've published, only three are truly historical. Only a few days ago, when working on this text, it struck me that all three have Paris as a primary setting. Moreover, all three are set against the backdrop of war. *The Shadow Of The Mole*, for instance—my latest novel, published in Dutch and very recently translated into English—takes place in France during World War I. Thinking about it, I have realized that I've written all my historical novels against the canvas of war to cope with my own experiences during the period—1990 until 2004—that I was a travel writer in conflict zones. Those years have made a lasting impact on me. I realize now that I needed the voyage back in time and the change of location to be able to write cogently about the atrocities of war, civil war, and social violence—but without compromising my peace of mind and plunging back too deep in my personal past. Through the filter of history, I'm able to analyze the events in a society that, regardless of the epoch, lead inevitably to conflict, and to highlight "la condition humaine," as Malraux put it, that plays such an important part in our aggressiveness toward others. Writing about past wars, I also write about myself in a veiled way, and with far less chance to hurt myself emotionally. Furthermore, a historical novel gives me the opportunity to comment on the present without being outdated by the rush of events in our time. Playwright and author Hubert O'Hearn puts it like this: "It has long been my suspicion that when a socially and politically clued-in writer sets his narrative in the past, it is because she or he actually intends to reveal the present while avoiding the turgid mud of active political discussion with all its ongoing presidents, organizations, media and headlines. Nothing ages quite so quickly as a novel set in the present day. The past exhibits a far more provocative analysis of the present than the actual present can ever hope to achieve."

I've always been fascinated by the mysterious relationship between our brain and our fragmentized conscience, and by the decidedly misty boundaries between what we call reality and delusion. This is the main theme of my novel *The Shadow Of The Mole*. As often, my own experiences planted the seed for this novel. One of the characters in *The Mole*—a mysterious gypsy drummer—is a challenging one. Does he really exist? Is he human or just a presence? Is he a product, caused by the horrors of war, of the deluded mind of a psychiatric patient, or does he really have influence on the course of history, as is suggested?

All the time when I was writing *The Shadow Of The Mole* I was thinking, "Am I not going too far? Creating a character like that means undertaking a journey into madness." But, you see, I'd once been haunted by a "mad" presence in one of the *favelas* (slums) of Manaus, the biggest "Amazon city" of Brazil. My guide Fuinha—his favorite expression was *Merda attingiu o ventilador*, or "the shit hits the fan"—wanted to bring me in contact with a *Paale*, a master in *macumba*, the sorcery that originated in Africa and that can show us *m'fa*: the world behind the trickery of this world. I didn't believe a word of Fuinha's ramblings, but thought it could be a fascinating anthropological theme, so I went with him at night into a dangerous shantytown. And that night, in spite of all reasoning and Western common sense, in a measly shack of an old black man who showed signs of what we call psychosis, I was confronted with something that was subtly inhuman. The sight of it, the message it seemed to convey, has burned itself in the deepest layers of my mind.

I've tried to create such a specter—an oracle from another plane of existence, if you like—as a main character in *The Shadow Of The Mole*. I suggest that this creature is one of the driving forces behind World War I. Is this true? It's easy to answer: of course not. Yet you can also say: *why not?* In the end, that isn't important. Among others, I think the meaningful aspects of *The Shadow Of The Mole* are the emotional charge of the search for the subsurface roots of our complex emotions and the metaphorical imagery of our dreams and delusions. The great Russian writer Gogol wrote, "Those of so-called sane mind are challenged by the wisdom of the insane." I think that has been true in all our history, so no wonder I used an historical setting for this metaphysical theme. For in the past lie the keys to our future, and in what is incomprehensible (read: insane) lurks the challenging path to the center of our being.

⌇

BOB VAN LAERHOVEN has written more than 30 books in Holland and Belgium, becoming well known for kaleidoscopic novels in which the fate of the individual is closely related to broad social transformations. Van Laerhoven's freelance writing and work for Médecins Sans Frontières (Doctors Without Borders) International has brought him to places of conflict, including Somalia, Liberia, Sudan, Gaza, Iran, Iraq, Myanmar, and the city of Sarajevo, some of which appear in his novels. The 2007 winner of the Hercule Poirot Prize for *Baudelaire's Revenge*, his latest work published in English is the short story collection *Dangerous Obsessions*. Find out more about Bob at www.bobvanlaerhoven.be.

JOSA YOUNG

~

Sail Upon the Land

*J*started writing *Sail Upon the Land* without any sense that
I was writing a historical novel. For me the past is so close
that it seems like the present, so exploring up and down
family trees feels normal. I come from families on both sides that
spent time tracing their path back up the centuries. I feel I know
personally many of the oddballs, writers, artists, heroes and inno-
vators—women and men—who squat and rustle in the branches of
my family tree.

At the same time it annoys me very much when people talk snob-
bishly about "coming from an ancient family" and priding themselves
on it. It is just luck where we come from, and the human family is
the most ancient and universal of all. We can trace ourselves back to
mitochondrial Eve standing up and surveying the African horizon.
And everyone has ancient roots, often close to where they currently
live. After all, when they dug up a 2000-year-old skeleton in Somerset's Mendip Hills and tested his DNA, they found more than one

descendent still living close by. Clouds of glory can often obscure pretty awful behavior in the so called "great" families—particularly the origins of their wealth and titles, which can include any or all of being the King's mistress, owning slaves, exploiting the poor and being generally appalling human beings. At the same time, I am interested in class and its conventions, and how it shapes and affects us, traps us in behavior that is not going to make us happy. I hope that the modern world and its great explosion in communication will help us to feel more like a human family as time goes on, and remember that we have so much more in common than anything else.

I am writing this in bed and in the corner of my eye is a chair. It is quite roughly made, not finely carved at all. It is probably 16th- or 17th-century country furniture. Bottoms that share my genes have sat on it since it was made. It came from a house in Kent built by an ancestor in the reign of Edward VI. As Edward only reigned for a short while, it was quite difficult to build a whole house in that time, but my ancestor managed it. The house is now an American college, and all around it 1930s terraces lap like utilitarian waves against the rocks of a glorious past. The house is a castle in its structure, but built of brick so useless for defense. I love houses and their history, and this house among others—long since swept out of family possession by war, death, loss and history simply moving on—was in my mind as I began to write *Sail Upon the Land*.

Some of my ancestors have lived in India for hundreds of years, marrying the local ladies in the early 17th century, as there were few English ladies there at that time. Being "Anglo-Indian" meant exactly that, being a hybrid. So I feel that duality too. When I was 25, I couldn't wait to travel to India, using some redundancy money from a job that had ended. When I arrived I felt more relaxed than ever before in my adult life. I loved every thing and every minute and spent six months observing a modern India that was balanced on layers and layers of incomers, invaders, traders and other cultures, all existing alongside one another in a strange harmony.

One day I was re-reading the part of *A Midsummer Night's Dream* in which Fairy Queen Titania speaks about her changeling Indian boy. I love that speech, which illustrates Titania's status as a fairy in one place (Greece, which in the play is really Shakespeare's England) and a goddess in another (India). In her speech, Titania is telling us where her little Indian boy came from: he is the child of her late votaress or priestess, who also is described as a friend. Shakespeare gets the feminine viewpoint exactly right in this speech— the kind of teasing, slightly salacious way that women talk to each other about sex and men and pregnancy. The Indian boy is the fulcrum of the plot. Oberon wants him, while Titania doesn't want to give him up. So my mind hovered over the little Indian boy and my own story began to form.

Sail Upon the Land doesn't follow *A Midsummer Night's Dream* in any linear or obvious way, but thinking about the play informed the fiction that was weaving in my mind. The commanding female figure of Hyppolyta and her heroic past and happy future. The lost lovers in the woods. The delusion of romantic love: It is all there, with human constants that persist through the centuries unchanged. I strive to write about people. Times may change but people don't, fundamentally.

The priestess "sails upon the land," her pregnant belly under her sari swelling like a sail in the wind. It is a beautiful visual metaphor, so that is what I wanted to call this novel that didn't exist yet. As I wrote, my mind flickered through women's radically changing experiences throughout the 20th century: freedom during both wars and confinement to a domestic role afterwards, which led to the backlash of the 1960s and 1970s. I wanted to write about how being a mother changed. I wanted to show how fluid class is in England. I wanted to try and convey some of my feelings about India and its past, and the visceral tug many British people still feel towards it.

In the end, though, *Sail Upon the Land* is centrally about being a mother. I poured many of my thoughts and feelings about my own maternal experience, along with my mother's and those of many other mothers I imagine or know, into a narrative that rolls through 80 years, dipping into lives and telling a circular story about how people affect each other by their actions. We often think we are alone, that what we do has no impact on others. But we are not alone.

As my ancestor John Donne (I am descended from his daughter Margaret) says:

> No man is an island, entire of itself; every man is a piece of the continent, a part of the main. If a clod be washed away by the sea, Europe is the less, as well as if a promontory were, as well as if a manor of thy friend's or of thine own were: any man's death diminishes me, because I am involved in mankind, and therefore never send to know for whom the bell tolls; it tolls for thee.

It is an honor and a privilege to be able to learn from my ancestor, however far off in time he is from me. I feel the need to live up to the departed in my family tree. I must write as well as I can and not embarrass them by being a "rubbish" person, writer, poet or novelist.

I must be brave and deal with my life in an honorable way, whatever happens, or I will let them down.

So that is the inspiration behind *Sail Upon the Land,* my sense that the past is always there. Time is real but also not real. I can touch the past in my home, in the form of inanimate objects, and in my heart, though grief and regret for the sad fate of so many of my relations, killed in wars, dying unnecessarily, being unhappy in their marriages. Nothing protects you from grief—not money, class, status, or anything else. Being human and loving opens us to sorrow, joy and all the best things in life, as there cannot be one without the other. Gazing at old family photographs—happy children, relaxed adults—and knowing their ends, gives me deep pangs of feeling. And this is why I am driven to write, to express those feelings.

~

JOSA YOUNG was born in her mother's four-poster bed in Kent, England, deep in a countryside scattered with cherry orchards and hop gardens. When she was packed off to boarding school at the age of seven, she found she could read as well as devour pictures to feed her imagination. The next ten years were spent deep in a book. Since studying English at Cambridge University, she has had several careers—in magazines, newspapers, the Internet, advertising and marketing—but her first love is fiction. Her first novel , *One Apple Tasted,* was published by Elliott & Thompson in 2009. *Sail Upon the Land* launched in 2014. Find Josa online at www.josayoungauthor.com.

CONTRIBUTOR INFORMATION

FRANCES BRODY has written eight mysteries set in the 1920s featuring elegant and intrepid Kate Shackleton, a World War I widow-turned-sleuth. *Murder in the Afternoon* was named a *Library Journal* best book. A 2016 Mary Higgins Clark finalist for *A Woman Unknown*, Frances began her writing career in BBC Radio and Television. She is the author of three sagas. The first saga, *Sisters on Bread Street*, based on her mother's stories, won the HarperCollins Elizabeth Elgin Award. Frances lives in Yorkshire, England, the setting for her novels. Find out more about Frances at www.frances-brody.com.

ELIZABETH BRUNDAGE graduated from Hampshire College, attended NYU film school, was a screenwriting fellow at the American Film Institute in Los Angeles, and received an M.F.A. as well as a James Michener Award from the University of Iowa Writers' Workshop. She has taught at a variety of colleges and universities, most recently at Skidmore College, where she was visiting writer-in-residence. *All Things Cease to Appear* is her fourth novel. She lives near Albany in upstate New York. Find her at www.elizabethbrundage.com.

~

MEGAN CHANCE is the critically acclaimed, award-winning author of several novels. Her books have been chosen for Borders Original Voices, Booksense and Amazon Books of the Month, and translated into several languages. Girlposse.com calls her a "writer of extraordinary talent," and Booklist calls her work "provocative and haunting." A former television news photographer with a B.A. from Western Washington University, Megan lives in the Pacific Northwest with her husband and two daughters. Find her at www.meganchance.com.

~

GARY CORBY is the author of the long-running Athenian Mystery series, starring Nicolaos, his girlfriend, Diotima, and his irritating 12-year-old brother, Socrates. Gary lives in Sydney, Australia, with his wife, two daughters, two ducks, two budgerigars, and a brush turkey that is almost as irritating as Socrates. He blogs at www.garycorby.com on all things ancient, Athenian, and mysterious.

~

GLEN CRANEY holds graduate degrees from Indiana University School of Law and Columbia University Graduate School of Journalism. He practiced trial law before joining the Washington, DC, press corps to cover national politics and the Iran-Contra

trial for *Congressional Quarterly* magazine. The Academy of
Motion Pictures Arts and Sciences awarded him the Nicholl
Fellowship prize for best new screenwriting. He is also a two-time
indieBRAG Medallion Honoree, a Chaucer Award First-Place
Winner for Historical Fiction set during the Middle Ages, and
has three times been named a *Foreword Reviews* Book-of-the-Year
Award Finalist. His novels have taken readers to the Scotland of
Robert Bruce, to Portugal during the Age of Discovery, to the
trenches of France during World War I, and to the American
Hoovervilles of the Great Depression. He lives in southern
California. His website is www.glencraney.com.

ROSEMARY DRONCHI is the author of the Rossini Trilogy
novels: *Blood Feud*, which appeared in 2012; *Retribution*,
published in summer 2014; and the upcoming *Redemption*. In
addition to the Trilogy, her works include a number of short
articles, the award-winning short story *Play for Keeps*, and the
contemporary novel *Of Body and Soul*, published under the pen
name L.J. Valentine. A professional hairstylist for most of her
working life, Rosemary used the stories of her Italian family as
inspiration for the novels. Though both grew up in Albany, NY,
Rosemary now lives with her husband Tony in Vero Beach, FL,
where she has recently retired from owning the Park Place Salon
& Spa. Find her online at www.rossinitrilogy.com.

ELLEN FELDMAN, a 2009 Guggenheim fellow, is the author of *Terrible Virtue, The Unwitting, Next to Love, Scottsboro* (shortlisted for the Orange Prize), *The Boy Who Loved Anne Frank* (translated into nine languages), and *Lucy.* She writes both fiction and social history, has published numerous book reviews, and has lectured extensively around the country and in Germany and England. Ellen grew up in northern New Jersey and attended Bryn Mawr College, from which she holds a B.A. and an M.A. in modern history. After further graduate studies at Columbia University, she worked for a New York publishing house. Ellen lives in New York City and East Hampton, NY, with her husband and a terrier named Charlie. Find Ellen online at www.ellenfeldman.com.

Author, book consultant and publisher **SUZANNE FOX** is the creative director of Stories of You Books and the founder/editor of the online journal *Society Nineteen,* which interviews contemporary authors writing about 19th-century experience. Her books include the memoir *Home Life: A Journey of Rooms and Recollections,* which was published by Simon and Schuster and selected as an Editor's Choice by the *Chicago Tribune,* and women's fiction that has been published under two different pseudonyms and translated into seven languages. A frequent teacher and speaker on writing, stories and creativity, Suzanne earned her M.F.A. from Columbia University and is currently working on a novel set in 19th-century Britain. Find out more at www.storiesofyou.org and www.bookstrategy.com.

~

NATALIE S. HARNETT has an M.F.A. from Columbia and has been awarded an Edward Albee Fellowship, a Summer Literary Seminars Fellowship, and a Vermont Studio Center Writer's Grant. Her fiction has been a finalist for the Mary McCarthy Prize, the Mid-List Press First Series Award for the Novel, the Glimmer Train's Short Story Award for New Writers, and The Ray Bradbury Short Story Fellowship. Her work has appeared in the *Chicago Quarterly Review*, the *Irish Echo*, the *Madison Review*, *The MacGuffin* and the *New York Times*. Her debut novel, *The Hollow Ground*, won the 2015 John Gardner Fiction Book Award and the 2014 Appalachian Book of the Year Award and was long-listed for the 2016 International Dublin Literary Award. She lives in Long Island and Northeastern PA with her husband and child. Find out more at www.natalieharnett.com.

~

BRUCE HOLSINGER is an award-winning novelist and scholar of the medieval period. His debut novel, *A Burnable Book*, won the John Hurt Fisher Prize, was named a *New York Times Book Review* Editor's Choice, and was shortlisted by the American Library Association for Best Crime Novel of 2014. His second novel, *The Invention of Fire*, received starred reviews in *Publisher's Weekly* and *Library Journal* and was named an Amazon Book of the Month for April 2015. His essays and reviews have appeared in publications including the *New York Times*, the *New York Review of Books*, *Slate*, and the *Washington Post*, and he appears regularly on NPR. A member of the faculty of the University of Virginia, he is the recipient of Guggenheim, American Council of Learned Societies and National Endowment for the Humanities fellowships. Find him online at www.bruceholsinger.com.

Born in Ireland, **ANDREW HUGHES** was educated at Trinity College, Dublin. It was while researching his acclaimed social history of Fitzwilliam Square—*Lives Less Ordinary: Dublin's Fitzwilliam Square, 1798-1922*—that he first came across the true story of John Delahunt, which inspired his debut novel. Andrew's second novel, *The Coroner's Daughter*, will appear in the UK in February 2017. Andrew lives in Dublin.

J. SYDNEY JONES is the author of numerous books of fiction and nonfiction, including the novels of the critically acclaimed Viennese Mystery series: *The Empty Mirror, Requiem in Vienna, The Silence, The Keeper of Hands, A Matter of Breeding* and *The Third Place.* He lived for many years in Vienna and has written several other books about the city, including the narrative history *Hitler in Vienna: 1907-1913,* the popular walking guide *Viennawalks,* and the thriller *Time of the Wolf.* Jones is also the author of the stand-alone thrillers *Ruin Value: A Mystery of the Third Reich* (2013), *The German Agent* (2014), and *Basic Law* (2015). He has lived and worked as a correspondent and freelance writer in Paris, Florence, Molyvos, and Donegal, and currently resides with his wife and son on the coast of central California. Visit him at jsydneyjones.com.

⌒

M. R. C. KASASIAN is the author of the Gower Street Detective Books: *The Mangle Street Murders, The Curse of the House of Foskett, Death Descends on Saturn Villa,* and *The Secrets of Gaslight Lane.* He lives with his wife in England. Follow him on Twitter at @MRCKASASIAN.

⌒

PHILIP KAZAN is the pseudonym of British author Pip-Vaughan Hughes, the author of the four Brother Petroc novels set in the 13th century. *The Painter of Souls* is his first book to be published in the US.

⌒

JENNIFER KINCHELOE is a research scientist turned writer of historical fiction. She earned a Masters degree in Public Health from Loma Linda University and a Ph.D. in Health Services from UCLA. She adores kickboxing, yoga, and developing complex statistical models. She was on the faculty at UCLA, where she spent 11 years conducting research to inform health policy. She currently lives in Denver, Colorado, with her husband and two children. *The Secret Life of Anna Blanc* is her first novel. For more information, visit her website at www.jenniferkincheloe.com and her Pinterest page (where thousands of images related to the book and its time period can be found) at www.pinterest.com/jrobin66.

⌒

⌒

DERYN LAKE is the pseudonym of well-known historical novelist Dinah Lampitt. Her historical mystery series featuring Apothecary John Rawlings now numbers sixteen titles. She also writes a contemporary mystery series featuring the Reverend Nick Lawrence; like the John Rawlings books, the Nick Lawrence books—*The Mills of God*, *Dead on Cue* and *The Moonlit Door*— are published by Severn House. She lives near Hastings in East Sussex in the UK. Find out more about the author and her books at www.derynlake.com.

⌒

DEBORAH LAWRENSON spent her childhood moving around the world with diplomatic service parents, from Kuwait to China, Belgium, Luxembourg and Singapore. She read English literature at Cambridge University and worked as a journalist in London. Many of her novels are set in and around the Mediterranean Sea. *The Lantern* was published to critical acclaim in the US, was chosen for Channel 4's The TV Book Club Summer Reads in the UK, and shortlisted for Romantic Novel of the Year 2012. She divides her time between rural Kent and a crumbling hamlet in Provence, the atmospheric setting for *The Lantern*. Her latest novel is *300 Days of Sun*. Find her online at www.deborah-lawrenson.co.uk.

⌒

Born and raised in Florida, GENE LEE currently lives in Indian River County. His plans to become a lawyer were derailed when at the age of 13, inspired by Ernest Hemingway and James Joyce, he began writing stories. After many years of writing and publishing his poetry in literary journals, Gene returned to his first love, fiction. *Men Without Hate*, his first novel, will appear from Neverland Publishing in 2017. Find out more about Gene and the book at www.geneleeauthor.com.

JOAN LENNON is a Scottish-Canadian/Canadian-Scottish writer who lives in the top two floors of a Victorian house looking out over the River Tay. She has had novels, stories and poems published for readers of all ages. Her latest young adult novel, *Silver Skin*, is a sci-fi historical adventure romance set in Skara Brae, Orkney, mostly in the time when the Stone Age was bleeding messily into the Bronze Age. Joan is a member of The History Girls blog; more information on her and the book can be found at www.joanlennon.co.uk.

MICHELLE LOVRIC's novels are always set at least partially in Venice. Her third novel, *The Remedy*, a mystery set against the background of 18th-century quack medicine, was long-listed for the Orange Prize. Her latest adult novels, *The Book of Human Skin* and *The True & Splendid History of the Harristown Sisters*, were published by Bloomsbury. Her novels for children, *The Undrowned Child* and *The Mourning Emporium* (Orion), feature the vengeful ghost of Venetian nobleman Baiamonte Tiepolo as their villain. They were followed by *Talina in the Tower* and *The Fate in the Box*. Find out more at www.michellelovric.com.

⁓

SARAH MCCOY is the *New York Times, USA Today*, and international bestselling author of *The Mapmaker's Children; The Baker's Daughter*, a 2012 Goodreads Choice Award Best Historical Fiction nominee; the novella "The Branch of Hazel," featured in the anthology *Grand Central*; and *The Time It Snowed in Puerto Rico*. Sarah's work has been featured in *Real Simple, The Millions*, the *Huffington Post*, and other publications. She has taught English writing at Old Dominion University and at the University of Texas at El Paso. She calls Virginia home but presently lives in El Paso, Texas. Find out more about Sarah at www.sarahmccoy.com.

⁓

Born into an army family, **JAMES MCGEE** grew up in Gibraltar, Germany and Northern Ireland. He has worked in banking, newspaper sales and the airline industry—for both British Airways and Pan Am—and as a store manager for two of Britain's leading booksellers. The five novels in the Hawkwood series are *Hawkwood, Resurrectionist, Rapscallion, Rebellion* and *The Blooding*. His other novels are *Trigger Men, Crow's War* and *Wolf's Lair*. When not involved in philosophical discourse with his laptop, he loves movies, travel and Bruce Springsteen, but not necessarily in that order. He lives in Somerset, England. Find out more at www.jamesmcgee.uk.

~

CINDY RINAMAN MARSCH has taught writing in colleges and online to secondary students for over 30 years before beginning her own writing career. She and her physics professor husband Glenn have raised and educated their four grown children and enjoy their garden and hobby winery in Western Pennsylvania. *Rosette: A Novel of Pioneer Michigan* (January 2016) is her first published work. Find out more at www.rosettebook.com.

~

MIRANDA MILLER has published seven novels, most recently *Loving Mephistopheles* (2006), *Nina in Utopia* (2010) and *The Fairy Visions of Richard Dadd* (2013). *King of the Vast*, the final volume of her Bedlam Trilogy, will be published in 2016. She has also published a volume of short stories and a book of interviews with homeless women and politicians. Her next novel will be set in the art world in 18th-century Rome and London. She blogs for The History Girls and works for The Literary Consultancy as a reader and mentor. She has a daughter and two stepchildren and lives in London with her second husband. Her website is www.mirandamiller.info.

~

JUDITH CLAIRE MITCHELL is the author of the novels *The Last Day of the War* and *A Reunion of Ghosts*. She teaches undergrad and graduate fiction workshops at the University of Wisconsin, where she is a professor of English and the director of the M.F.A. program in creative writing. She has received grants and fellowships from the Michener-Copernicus Society of America, the Wisconsin Institute for Creative Writing, the Wisconsin Arts Board, and Bread Loaf, among others. Find out more at www.judithclairemitchell.com.

~

CHRIS NICKSON was born and raised in Leeds. He has a love affair with the city, exploring it in fiction over several different periods. A crime writer and music journalist, he spent 30 years in the US, many in Seattle, before returning to the UK, finally settling contentedly just a mile from where he grew up. In novels he writes the places and people he feels in his bones. With music he prefers the paths that aren't as well trodden, that lead to other parts of the globe. Find out more about Chris's work at www.chrisnickson.co.uk.

~

Award-winning author **J.L. OAKLEY** writes historical fiction that spans the mid-19th century to World War II. Her novels include *The Tree Soldier*, set in the Pacific Northwest during the 1930s, and *Timber Rose*, as well as *The Jøssing Affair*. Recent recognition includes a 2015 Silver WILLA Literary Award for historical fiction. When not writing, she demonstrates 19th-century folkways to school-age children at national parks and museums. Find out more at www.historyweaver.wordpress.com.

CHARLES PALLISER was born in Massachusetts but has lived in the UK since the age of three. A graduate of Oxford University, he writes full time in London. His debut novel, *The Quincunx*, became an international bestseller and was awarded the Sue Kaufman Prize for First Fiction by the American Academy and Institute of Arts and Letters, given for the best first novel published in North America. His subsequent books include *The Sensationist, Betrayals, The Unburied*, and *Rustication*, which appeared in 2013 and was chosen as one of *Publishers Weekly's* Best Books of the Year.

ALYSSA PALOMBO is a recent graduate of Canisius College, with degrees in English and creative writing. A passionate music lover, she is a classically trained vocalist as well as a big fan of heavy metal. *The Violinist of Venice* is her first novel. She lives in Buffalo, New York. Her website is www.alyssapalombo.com.

ANN PARKER earned degrees in Physics and English Literature before falling into a career as a science writer. The only thing more fun for her than slipping oblique Yeats references into a fluid dynamics article is delving into the past. Her Silver Rush historical mystery series is set in the silver boomtown of Leadville, Colorado, in the early 1880s and has been picked as a "Booksellers Favorite" by the Mountains and Plains Independent Booksellers

Association. A member of Mystery Writers of America and
Women Writing the West, Ann lives with her husband and an
uppity cat near Silicon Valley, whence they have weathered
numerous high-tech boom-and-bust cycles. Find Ann online at
www.annparker.net.

~

ELIOT PATTISON is the author of eight Inspector Shan
mysteries, most lately *Soul of the Fire*. *The Skull Mantra*, which
debuted the series, won the Edgar Award and was a finalist for the
Gold Dagger. He is also the author of the Bone Rattler mystery
series, set in the mid-18th century, and the post-apocalyptic
mystery novel *Ashes of the Earth*. An international lawyer by
training, Pattison is a world traveler who has spoken and written
extensively on international issues. Pattison resides in rural
Pennsylvania with his wife, three children, two horses, and two
dogs on a colonial-era farm. For more information on the author
and books, visit www.eliotpattison.com.

~

SUE PURKISS has published three books for young readers; a
contemporary novel, *The Willow Man*; and two historical novels.
The first of these, *Warrior King*, is a re-imagining of the story of
Alfred the Great, partly told through the eyes of his daughter.
Emily's Surprising Voyage, Sue's most recent book, is again for
younger readers, and is set on Brunel's beautiful ship, the SS
Great Britain. Sue's story about Alfred the Great's daughter

Aethelflaed appears in *The Daughters of Time*, an anthology of stories by the authors of The History Girls blog. Find Sue online at www.suepurkiss.blogspot.co.uk and www.the-history-girls. blogspot.com.

~

CELIA REES has written over 20 books in different genres but is perhaps best known for her historical fiction. Her first historical novel, *Witch Child*, was translated into 28 languages. *Witch Child* and subsequent titles, *Sorceress* and *Pirates!*, were shortlisted for the Guardian, Whitbread (Costa) and W.H. Smith Awards in the UK and won awards in the UK, USA, France and Italy. Her latest book, the dark contemporary thriller *This is Not Forgiveness*, was nominated for several UK awards and was one of *Kirkus Reviews'* Best Teen Books of 2012. She lives in Leamington Spa and divides her time between writing, talking to readers in schools and libraries, and reviewing and teaching creative writing. Find her at www.celiarees.com and www.the-history-girls.blogspot.com.

~

ELIZABETH ROSNER is a novelist, poet, and essayist living in Berkeley, California. Her third novel, *Electric City*, was named among the best books of 2014 by National Public Radio. Her acclaimed poetry collection, *Gravity*, was also published in 2014. *The Speed of Light*, Rosner's 2001 debut novel, was translated into nine languages. Short-listed for the Prix Femina, the book won several literary prizes in both the US and Europe, including the Prix France Bleu Gironde; the Great Lakes Colleges Award for

New Fiction; and Hadassah Magazine's Ribalow Prize, judged by Elie Wiesel. *Blue Nude*, Rosner's second novel, was selected as one of the *San Francisco Chronicle's* best books of 2006. Her essays, poems and book reviews are widely published in leading periodicals. Find out more at www.elizabethrosner.com.

STEVEN SAYLOR is the author of the Roma Sub Rosa® series of historical mysteries featuring Gordianus the Finder and set in the ancient Rome of Cicero, Caesar, and Cleopatra. The latest novels in the series—*The Seven Wonders, Raiders of the Nile,* and *Wrath of the Furies*—are prequels about Gordianus in his youth. Steven is also the author of two novels set in his native Texas and the international bestsellers *Roma: The Novel of Ancient Rome* and *Empire: The Novel of Imperial Rome,* two novels comprising a multi-generational saga that spans the first 1200 years of the city. A third novel in this series is currently in the research stage. He divides his time between homes in Berkeley, California, and Austin, Texas. Find Steven online at www.stevensaylor.com.

SOPHIE SCHILLER was born in Paterson, NJ and grew up in the West Indies. Among other oddities her family tree contains a Nobel prize-winning physicist and a French pop singer. She loves stories that carry the reader back in time to exotic and far-flung locations. She was educated at American University in Washington, DC and lives in Brooklyn. In addition to *Transfer*

Day, she is the author of *Race to Tibet*, a high-altitude adventure and survival story set in the world's most forbidden country. She is currently working on *Island of Eternal Fire*, a historical thriller set in Martinique during the deadliest volcanic disaster of the 20th century. Find Sophie online at www.sophieschiller.blogspot. com.

⁓

CAM TERWILLIGER's fiction and narrative journalism can be found online in *American Short Fiction, Electric Literature, The Rumpus*, and *Narrative*, the latter of which named him one of "15 Under 30." In print, his writing appears in *West Branch, Post Road*, and *Gettysburg Review*, among others. His work has been supported by fellowships and scholarships from the Fulbright Program, the James Jones First Novel Fellowship, the Massachusetts Cultural Council, the Virginia Center for Creative Arts, and the Bread Loaf, Tin House, and Sewanee Writers' Conferences. He teaches at Drew University and lives in Brooklyn, New York. Find him online at www.camterwilliger.com.

⁓

JANET TODD has worked as an academic in Ghana, Puerto Rico, the US, Scotland, India and England. Until recently, she was President of Lucy Cavendish College, University of Cambridge, where she established the Lucy Cavendish Fiction Prize. She has been a critic and editor as well as a biographer of Jane Austen, Aphra Behn (in a biography shortly to be reissued), and Mary Wollstonecraft and her daughters. Recently she has become a novelist with two works, *A Man of Genius*, set in Venice and Regency London, and Lady Susan Plays the Game, a spinoff from a Jane Austen novella. Her website is www.janettodd.co.uk.

~

BOB VAN LAERHOVEN has written more than 30 books in Holland and Belgium, becoming well known for kaleidoscopic novels in which the fate of the individual is closely related to broad social transformations. Van Laerhoven's freelance writing and work for Médecins Sans Frontières (Doctors Without Borders) International has brought him to places of conflict, including Somalia, Liberia, Sudan, Gaza, Iran, Iraq, Myanmar, and the city of Sarajevo, some of which appear in his novels. The 2007 winner of the Hercule Poirot Prize for *Baudelaire's Revenge*, his latest work published in English is the short story collection Dangerous Obsessions. Find out more about Bob at www.bobvanlaerhoven.be.

~

JOSA YOUNG was born in her mother's four-poster bed in Kent, England, deep in a countryside scattered with cherry orchards and hop gardens. When she was packed off to boarding school at the age of seven, she found she could read as well as devour pictures to feed her imagination. The next ten years were spent deep in a book. Since studying English at Cambridge University, she has had several careers—in magazines, newspapers, the Internet, advertising and marketing—but her first love is fiction. Her first novel , *One Apple Tasted,* was published by Elliott & Thompson in 2009. *Sail Upon the Land* launched in 2014. Find Josa online at www.josayoungauthor.com.

~

ACKNOWLEDGMENTS

First and foremost, our profound appreciation goes to the 38 authors who contributed to this volume. It quite literally would not exist without them, and to each we extend our deepest thanks.

It takes a (virtual) village to create a book, and the talented team that worked on the production side of this anthology did impeccable work transforming it from manuscript to final product.

CJ Madigan of Shoebox Stories has brought her keen eye, book design expertise, and systems savvy to the design and production of this book as well as to the visualization of everything else "So You." She is a painstaking, energizing, and inspiring collaborator.

Ruth Elkin and Cindy Rinaman Marsch have proofread with patience, skill, and care; Mikki Lusquinos has done valiant work on various tasks including on exhausted-editor morale; and Linda Gordon Hengerer has been invaluable on marketing issues. Tom Leonard, Chad Leonard, Cynthia Callander, and the rest of the team at the

222

~

Vero Beach Book Center offer the inspiration of great author and book events and a model of what independent bookstores can be.

Finally, our thanks to RedRemy for the evocative cover image. Like the best historical novels, it brings together the best of past and future, tradition and freshness.

COPYRIGHT AND PRIOR PUBLICATIONS

The essays appearing in this volume remain the copyright of their individual authors:

Frances Brody on *Sisters on Bread Street* © 2016 Frances Brody

Elizabeth Brundage on *All Things Cease to Appear* © 2016 by Elizabeth Brundage

Megan Chance on *The Fianna Trilogy* © 2016 by Megan Chance

Gary Gorby on *The Athenian Mysteries* © 2016 by Gary Corby

Glen Craney on *The Fire and the Light* © 2013 by Glen Craney

Rosemary Dronchi on *The Rossini Trilogy* © 2015 by Rosemary Dronchi

Ellen Feldman on *Terrible Virtue* © 2016 Ellen Feldman

Suzanne Fox on *The Shell House* © 2016 by Suzanne Fox

Natalie S. Harnett on *The Hollow Ground* © 2015 by Natalie S. Harnett

Bruce Holsinger on the John Gower Novels © 2015 Bruce Holsinger

Andrew Hughes on *The Convictions of John Delahunt* © 2015 by Andrew Hughes

J. Sydney Jones on the Viennese Mysteries © 2015 by J. Sydney Jones

M.R.C. Kasasian on the Gower Street Detective Books © 2015 by M.R.C. Kasasian

Philip Kazan on *The Painter of Souls* © 2015 by Philip Kazan

Jennifer Kincheloe on *The Secret Life of Anna Blanc* © 2015 by Jennifer Kincheloe

Deryn Lake on the John Rawlings Mysteries © 2016 by Deryn Lake

Deborah Lawrenson on *300 Days of Sun* and Other Works © 2016 by Deborah Lawrenson

Gene Lee on *Men Without Hate* © 2016 by Gene Lee

Joan Lennon on *Silver Skin* © 2015 by Joan Lennon

Michelle Lovric on the Venetian Novels © 2016

Sarah McCoy on *The Mapmaker's Children* © 2014 Sarah McCoy

James McGee on *The Blooding* © 2015 James McGee

Cindy Rinaman Marsch on *Rosette* © 2016

Miranda Miller on *Loving Mephistopheles* © 2015 by Miranda Miller

Judith Claire Mitchell on *A Reunion of Ghosts* © 2015 by Judith Claire Mitchell

Chris Nickson on *Leeds: The Biography* © 2015 by Chris Nickson

J.L. Oakley on *The Jøssing Affair* © 2016 J.L. Oakley

Charles Palliser on *The Quincunx, The Unburied* and *Rustication* © 2015 Charles Palliser

Alyssa Palombo on *The Violinist of Venice* © 2015 Alyssa Palombo

Ann Parker on the Silver Rush Mysteries © 2016 by Ann Parker

Sue Purkiss on *Warrior King* © 2015 Sue Purkiss

Celia Rees on *Witch Child* and *Sorceress* © 2016 Celia Rees

Elizabeth Rosner on *Electric City* © 2015 Elizabeth Rosner

Steven Saylor on the Roma Sub Rosa Novels © 1993 Steven Saylor

Sophie Schiller on *Transfer Day* © 2016 Sophie Schiller

Cam Terwilliger on *Yet Wildnerness Grew in my Heart* © 2014 Cam Terwilliger

Janet Todd on *A Man of Genius* © 2016 Janet Todd

Bob van Laerhoven on *The Shadow of the Mole* © 2015 by Bob van Laerhoven

Josa Young on *Sail Upon the Land* © 2016 Josa Young

Glen Craney's essay first appeared in slightly different form in "Stories of Serendipity: Writing Historical Fiction Series Featuring Author Glen Craney" by Stephanie Renee Dos Santos on the website of the Historical Novel Society, September 22, 2013 (www.historicalnovelsociety.org).

Ellen Feldman's essay was originally published as "The Difficulty of Writing a Difficult Woman" in *Omnivoracious*, the Amazon Book Review, on March 28, 2016.

Bruce Holsinger's essay first appeared under the title "On Seeing (And Not Seeing) Medieval London" in the *Historical Novel Review* of the Historical Novel Society, Issue 73, August 2015 (www.historicalnovelsociety.org).

Sarah McCoy's essay first appeared as "Story Mapmakers, No GPS Required" on Writer Unboxed, October 28, 2014 (www. writerunboxed.com).

Judith Claire Mitchell's essay originally appeared as "The Book That Refused to Write Itself" on the Powell's Books blog, March 24, 2015 (www.powells.com).

Steven Saylor's essay was first published as "All Roads Led to Rome" Mystery Readers Journal, Volume 9 #2, Summer 1993 (www.mysteryreaders.org) and later collected in his *A Bookish Bent: Essays about Reading, Writing, and George W. Bush's Close Call on the Running Trail*, Roma Sub Rosa Press 2013.

Cam Terwilliger's essay first appeared as "Field Notes from a Fulbright Scholar: In Kahnawà:ke Territory" in *Electric Literature*, June 27, 2014 (www.electricliterature.com).

Janet Todd's essay first appeared in slightly longer form as a guest post on the blog of The Mitford Society, March 10, 2106 (wwww. themitfordsociety.wordpress.com).

ABOUT STORIES OF YOU BOOKS

As "the anthology people," we at Stories of You Books capture, share and celebrate the truths that can be found at the intersection of many compelling stories.

As custom anthology creators, we help each client identify and use their own organization's many powerful stories to engage members and markets, honor contribution, inspire action, and build and preserve priceless legacy.

As anthology publishers for the retail market, we conceive, curate, and publish impeccable, enduring anthologies characterized by intriguing topics, accomplished voices, and broad readership.

In all of our work, we try to balance innovative big-picture vision with impeccable attention to detail, and connect diverse individual perspectives not just to each other but also to shared human needs, values, experiences and dreams.

Are you an individual with insight or expertise to share? An organization seeking to deepen your impact, now and forever? A reader ready for fresh perspectives? If so, we hope you'll make us part of your journey.

For more information, including upcoming publications and calls for submissions, please visit us at www.storiesofyou.org.

OPPORTUNITIES FOR
EDITORS AND CONTRIBUTORS

Beginning in 2017, Stories of You Books will open some of its series to editorial proposals and some of its anthologies to contributor submissions. For information on upcoming editorial and contributor opportunities, please visit www.storiesofyou.org.

STORIES OF YOU BOOKS

www.ingramcontent.com/pod-product-compliance
Lightning Source LLC
Chambersburg PA
CBHW070917180626
46817CB00003B/1101